FATE KNOWS BEST

Kindred of Arkadia

ALANEA ALDER

Dedication

~Omnia Vincit Amor~ Love Conquers All~

To everyone who waited... the wait is over.

PROLOGUE

"WHY ARE WE HERE?" THE voice of the high-pitched hyena grated on his nerves. If only there was another way. The gentleman sighed. No. His kind weren't permitted in Arkadia, and this group had access.

"You are here because I require something from you," he said quietly.

"Who the fuck are you?" the hyena demanded, crossing his arms over his chest defiantly. The gentleman moved faster than he knew the shifter could track and appeared behind the man. He straightened his fingers and plunged his hand into the hyena's back, wrapping his fingers around the spine. The hyena's screams filled the room. The gentleman sighed happily.

"Shush or I will kill you," he warned softly. The hyena quieted down but kept whimpering.

"I bought the debt you incurred when you lost the last shipment meant for your associates. I work with them from time to time as well. They were most eager to take my money. So you see, that makes you my little puppet," he said, shaking the hand that was still fisted around the hyena's spine. The hyena's body jerked from side to side.

"Now, what I need is very simple. Totally within your capabilities to get. I almost feel like it's too easy for you. What I want is Arkadion blood," the gentleman said, savoring the name Arkadion on his tongue as if it were a fine wine.

"How do we get it?" the hyena asked gasping in pain.

"I don't care. Find a way. Bring me Arkadion blood or come back and face me," the gentleman said, ripping his hand out of the hyena. He brought his hand to his mouth and began to slowly lick his fingers.

"Face me or face the Arkadion. Now go," the gentleman said and then nodded to the large shadow in the corner.

The figure grabbed one hyena in each hand and took them from the room.

"Thank you, Payne," the gentleman said cheerfully as he continued to clean each digit.

CHAPTER ONE

"**M**ADE A WRONG TURN, ONCE or twice. Dug my way out, blood and fire." Rebecca sang along to P!nk as her bright-blue Smart car made its way down the dark mountain highway. She had ignored the small clanking sound she heard from her tiny car all the way through South Carolina, and it was now making itself known.

"Just get me to the closest city and I promise to get you the works. I'm talking new belts and detailing, just please don't leave me stranded in the middle of nowhere in the North Carolina mountains." Rebecca pleaded with her car. She glanced down realizing she was almost out of gas as well.

Afraid to pull over in case her car decided to cut off on her, she was scanning the GPS on her phone to find the closest town when a deer followed by a fairly large animal darted into the middle of the road. She slammed on her brakes, lost her grip on the phone and heard a dull thud as it landed. When her car came to a complete stop, she looked around to find neither animal was visible.

Breathing heavily and with shaking hands she retrieved her phone from under the gas pedal just in time to see the battery die.

"Oh come on, please!" She shook the phone as if that would breathe new life into the battery.

Looking out the window, she tried to recall what was close by. It wasn't hard to do. The nearest place, a rest stop, was about thirty miles away and forget about cities that would be another hundred miles of driving. She sighed as she saw one snowflake, then another hit her windshield. She glanced to her left and blinked. Was that road there a second ago? She squinted and could clearly see a well-kept paved road. On the horizon beyond the trees she saw the faint glow of lights. She was contemplating going down the unknown road when her car began to sputter. She quickly put it in gear deciding to take her chances with a nearby unknown rather than an impossible-to-reach certainty.

She drove down the dark road and was just about to turn around when she came upon an open archway. Hanging from the center of the arch was a sign that just read "Arkadia."

She frowned. *I don't remember an Arkadia on the map.* She shrugged pushing on the gas pedal to urge the car forward. The snow was really coming down now. As she looked around to get her bearings the gargoyles on the top of a large white building caught her attention. She felt a smile tug at her lips. The sign out front let her know it was used as the townhall, courthouse, and church among other things depending on the day.

Now that makes sense and is a perfect use of space.

The jukebox in the window of "Ma's Diner"

came into view as she continued.

I bet they have amazing food. She made a mental note to go back there for dinner.

When she came to an intersection she looked around trying to decide which way to go. She chuckled when she saw the aptly named electronics shop, "Johnny 5's".

She opted to go straight when there was no garage in sight down the other street. At the next intersection she looked right to see an old metal sign with "Garage" in large bold font. She shrugged.

I guess the name says it all.

She pulled in front of the open bay doors as her car decided to die with a loud bang. Sighing with relief that she had made it to civilization, she picked up the backpack that served as her purse and hopped out of her car, leaving her luggage in the back seat. A mountainous man stepped out of the open bay door wiping his hands on a rag. His shiny brown hair was going grey at the temples, kindness showed in his green eyes, and it seemed the light lines on his face were from smiling or laughing. For some reason, though they looked nothing alike, he reminded her of her father.

The man smiled warmly and walked up to her. "It's so tiny it looks like a toy!" the large man exclaimed as he walked slowly around the car.

"Right now it's a broken toy. It literally just died in your parking lot. Do you think you can fix it?" she asked.

The man just absently nodded and kept circling the car.

"You can leave it here and I will play with it. My name is Aaron Arkadion. This is my garage." He ran a hand over the hood as if he were petting the family dog.

"Thank you. My name is Rebecca. Rebecca Morgan."

When he finally looked up and really looked at her, she could see a flicker of shock in his eyes.

"How did you get here?" he asked.

Confused, she replied, "I drove here." He tilted his head and continued to look at her. She stared right back. Her stomach growled.

"Are you hungry?"

"I'm starved! My cheese crackers and beef jerky ran out sometime this afternoon."

"Come on, I'll drive you to my wife's diner. She makes the most amazing food, as you can see," he said, laughing and patting his mid-section.

"Oh no, I couldn't put you out like that. I can walk." She hefted her backpack up over her shoulder.

The large man smiled again pointing to the sky where the snow was coming down harder now. "It's no trouble. I was about to head there anyway for my own dinner. Come on, little one, let's go get something warm to eat." He easily plucked her backpack from her shoulder and walked over to a huge truck.

She shrugged and followed.

In the end he had to reach over the seat to pull her in, since the truck was so far off the ground.

"My dad used to call me that," she said, as she buckled her seat belt.

"What? Little one?"

She nodded.

"Used to?" he asked, in a gentle tone.

She nodded again as he pulled away from the garage. "He died a few years ago. There was a house fire. I lost him and the house. The only thing that made it was my car and only because it was with me at work at the time. Since then I've learned not to accumulate things." She watched as they passed the grocery store before making the left that put them back onto Main Street.

"I am sorry for your loss. It must have been hard. You have no other family?" he asked frowning, concern and worry etched on his face.

She shook her head. "Nope. Just me now. I lost my mother when I was three. She died in a car accident. They were both older when they had me, so I never knew my grandparents, and I was an only child, so no siblings. But it's okay. A lot of people don't have family." She turned her face from the window where she had been watching the small town go by to see his large green eyes filled with tears for her. Her eyes widened. "Oh! It's okay, really!" She patted his shoulder.

He sniffled loudly. "It's not right, a tiny thing like you being alone. Not right at all." He easily pulled into a parking spot near the door. The street was packed with cars. She was surprised no one had taken the spot so close until she spotted the sign.

Reserved for Pa.

"You wait there. I will come around for you," he said before exiting the truck.

She grinned as she watched him walk around the truck to open the door for her. He put his hands under her arms and easily lifted her out of the truck. She felt like a rag doll. Surprisingly despite his size, not once did she feel uncomfortable or afraid of him, but then again she had always been a good judge of character, and at the moment her gut was telling her she just made a really special friend. She tucked her hand into his elbow and let him escort her into the diner. She couldn't wait to see the menu. She was starved.

When they walked into the diner everyone immediately quieted. Rebecca realized that she was a stranger in what was a typical small town. The quiet part didn't bother her as much as the staring. It was making her feel like a bug under a microscope. She had started to edge behind her new friend when he wrapped an arm around her shoulders and pulled her to stand beside him.

"This is Rebecca Morgan. She is from out of town." He made from out of town sound as if she came from outer space.

"Rebecca, why don't you tell them how you found our small town." He walked her to the counter and lifted her up onto the bar stool. Her feet didn't even touch the metal bar halfway down the stool, so her feet swung freely. The black–and–white checkerboard floor gleamed as though it had just been waxed and the entire placed smelled of comfort foods and lemon cleaner.

Not one to be shy, she launched into her story.

"Well, I've been driving around for a while, kinda on a sabbatical since my jerk of a boss decided I was 'redundant.' Anyway, my car started making funny noises somewhere in South Carolina. So when the noises started getting louder tonight, I bargained with her that if she got me to civilization I would make sure she got new parts. Right after that I was checking my phone's GPS, which by the way, didn't even have your town showing, so I know the software must be outdated, but then again it was only a ninety-nine-cent app so what can you expect, right?" A few heads nodded.

"So I was checking my phone and when I looked up, a deer then this huge animal came darting out into the middle of the road. So I slammed on my brakes and my phone went flying. When I looked up both animals were gone. I'm glad I didn't hit them. I love animals." A lot of people were smiling.

"Any hosier, I picked up my phone, which immediately died. Then it began to snow and my car started stuttering. I was just about to cry when I saw out of the corner of my eye this road with a glow up ahead like a town or city. I could have sworn it wasn't there before. So I decided a well-kept road like that had to lead somewhere, so I chose to go after an unknown nearby place rather than walk the miles and miles to the next rest stop. I found the garage and then my poor car died. Mr. Arkadion here offered me a ride to the diner and here I am." She smiled waving her hand about, pointing to the diner.

A well-dressed man stood. He had reddish-brown hair and light amber eyes. He was a bit shorter than Mr. Arkadion and had a lean runner's build where the older man was more barrel-chested. Rebecca would have stared longer except there was also a pretty blonde woman sitting beside him. She was blonde and pretty, but field-hockey-player-blonde and pretty, not beach-blonde and pretty. Rebecca long ago differentiated between the two. The woman had an open smile and royal blue eyes which contrasted wonderfully with her honey-blonde hair. Rebecca thought about her boring brown hair and sighed.

The handsome man spoke. "You didn't know our town was here at all? You just followed the road?" Everyone turned their head back to Rebecca waiting on her answer. It seemed to be very important.

"No, I had no idea it was here, though I am very glad it was. I don't know what would have happened to me if I had to walk down the highway," she replied.

"I shudder to imagine what would have happened to a tiny thing like you." A warm female voice said from behind her. Rebecca turned to look at one of the most "mom" looking women she had ever met. She was also tall and her brown eyes were kind and felt like they knew all your secrets. She knew this woman could put a Band-Aid on your knee while baking a homemade pie, lecturing you on why you acted foolishly in the first place to earn the Band-Aid and still have dinner on the table and the house clean. This woman epitomized home and family and love.

"Bran, perhaps you can have someone check the perimeter, just in case there is a large animal out there on the loose," she said pointedly raising an eyebrow. The handsome man who had stood nodded then walked to the back of the diner on his cell phone. Rebecca got the feeling that wasn't exactly what she was trying to say, but for the life of her couldn't think of what else it could mean.

The motherly woman turned to Rebecca. "We've been having problems with hyenas lately. I'm Margaret Arkadion, but everyone around here calls me Ma. Now, young lady, what can I get you to eat?" She smiled widely.

"Get her something hearty, Margie. Poor little thing has no family or home. I don't think she's eaten right in months."

Rebecca looked up into Mr. Arkadion's face and could see his concern as plain as day. The man was truly the most caring person she had ever met. She glanced around the diner. Even though Mr. Arkadion spoke to his wife in a low tone, she could see the empathy in the townspeople's eyes as they looked at her. Her eyes started to water, a direct result of the most kindness she had been shown in a long time.

Ma's eyes went to Rebecca, and she reached out her hand to cup her cheek. Her rough work-worn fingers felt warm. "You're more than welcome here. If you need anything during your stay you come to me or Pa and we'll take care of it. Consider yourself under our care." She spoke the last sentence a little louder. Nearly every head in the diner nodded.

"Now let's see, something hearty huh. I think you'll like my homemade beef stew and baking-powder biscuits. It'll put some meat on those bones of yours." She clucked, shaking her head at how small she was.

Rebecca laughed. "I'm actually overweight for my height. I could stand to lose about fifteen pounds."

A man near the door snorted. Rebecca wheeled around and looked at him.

"What?" she asked.

"If you were any smaller we'd have to tie a bell around your neck like a kitten so we wouldn't step on you." He grinned cheekily.

The field-hockey-player blonde laughed out loud.

"Liam is right, honey, you are already tiny enough. My name is Kate Edwards. That is Bran McGregor. Bran and I," she pointed to the man who returned from making his phone call, "our family looks after the lands to the east of here. That is Liam Lewenhart," she said, pointing to the smiling man. He had short blond hair and an easy smile. He looked like he would be right at home on the beach relaxing. "Liam there, when he's not flirting, he and his family look after the lands to the west of town. The Arkadions, whom you've met, well the parents anyway, they look after the lands to the north."

"Who looks after the lands to the south?" Rebecca asked.

"To the south are two government-owned nature refuges. Wild animals live there. If you're ever lost, do not head south. It's dangerous, even at the borders," Liam explained. Pa nodded.

Rebecca turned to Bran. "Is that why Mrs. Arkadion is having you check the perimeters?" she asked.

Pa barked out a laugh. "Don't let her hear you call her Mrs. Arkadion. She believes that was my mother. You can call her Ma and me Pa. We're not real formal around here," Pa said, smiling down at her.

Bran nodded. "Something like that. We have a perimeter around the town to, uh, keep us safe. I sent two of my, uh, friends out to check and make sure that it was okay and to see if they could find tracks of the animal you saw."

"Here you are, pretty lady." A deep voice said from behind the counter. She turned to face yet another devastatingly handsome man. Was there something in the water that made these men drool-worthy?

"Thank you, Connor. Rebecca, this is Connor. He's my third-eldest son," Pa announced proudly.

Rebecca smiled and accepted a huge bowl of stew. Connor looked a lot like his father. She could see what Pa must have looked like when he was younger. They both had the same warm chestnut-brown hair and brilliant green eyes. She must have been blushing, because Kate spoke up.

"If you think he's cute, wait until you see all seven of them together. I swear if I weren't taken…" She let her voice trail off as Bran growled lowly and she laughed.

Rebecca's jaw dropped.

"There are seven of you?" she asked Connor. She shook her head and looked at Ma.

"You are one amazing woman," she said, shoveling a spoonful of stew in her mouth.

Connor just grinned. "Trust me, she was more than up to the task of having seven boys. She still keeps us on our toes."

"Good answer, son," Ma replied, wrapping an arm around his waist.

Rebecca smiled at their obvious love for one another.

Just as she was about to take a second bite the door opened and a blast of cold air blew in. A tall man stepped into the diner and took off his sheriff's hat.

He filled the doorway in height and breadth. She could only stare. Bran, Liam, and even Connor were handsome. But the man before her was a god. His broad muscled chest tapered down to a fit waist. The distinct shadow of a beard giving him a rugged look. His dark lashes matched the deep-brown hair he wore long, almost to his shoulders.

She placed a hand to her chest. It felt as if her very soul was reaching out to him. He looked down at her, his green eyes widening as he inhaled deeply. She watched in amazement as his eyes darken to a forest green. He growled low and long before stalking toward her.

Her breath caught in her throat as his face descended toward hers. When their lips met she felt her entire world shift on its axis. Fire raced through her body igniting small explosions. His hand in her hair pulled her closer. She opened her mouth for a whimper, and he took full advantage of it, sliding his tongue in past her lips to trace the roof of her mouth. She was just about to wrap her legs around his waist when he abruptly stood back, breathing heavily. He stared down at her as if seeing her for the first time. He opened his mouth, then closed it. Opened it again and closed it. Roughly he slammed his hat back on his head, turned, and stormed back out into the snow.

Out of the corner of her eye she saw Connor clear the counter with a one-handed jump to run after the man.

"Holy shit!" Liam exclaimed.

"That was my eldest son Aleksander," Pa said thoughtfully as he rubbed a hand over his chin.

"I need to go now. I need to walk my car." Rebecca jumped off the barstool, promptly falling to the floor as her knees gave out. "Your floor is broken. It moved closer to my head," she said in a daze.

"Good God!" Pa reached down, picked her up and held her like a baby doll. "Margie, I don't think she's okay," he said, looking into Rebecca's eyes. "Her pupils are completely dilated."

"Of course she isn't okay. Aleks all but started the claiming." Ma said untying her apron.

"Should you say that? She still doesn't know about us," Pa whispered, speaking over Rebecca's head.

"Right now that poor baby doesn't know up from down. Do you, baby girl?" she asked, rubbing a hand over Rebecca's curls.

"Yes, I'm upside down," Rebecca agreed as she desperately tried to make sense of their conversation.

Pa grimaced. "What the hell is that boy doing?" he asked no one in particular.

"At least we now know how she made it past the town's perimeter spell to keep out humans," Kate said.

"Never mind that now. Let's take her to Leona's. Her bed and breakfast is across the street. I would take her to the ranch, but with the way Aleks reacted..." Ma trailed off as she put on a light coat.

"Is that wise, Ma? Leona is a bit...out there. Bran and I could take her to our place," Kate volunteered.

"We can?" Bran asked and Kate elbowed him in the stomach.

"Of course we can," he confirmed, nodding.

Ma shook her head. "We appreciate the offer. But she'll be perfectly fine at the bed and breakfast. Leona is a bit high strung and loves shocking people with her eccentric ways, but I know she will take real good care of our baby girl here." Ma said as she opened the door. "Spread the word, Rebecca is to be protected at all costs."

Why? Rebecca wondered. *Because her son likes me? He didn't act like he liked me. Oh, it's still snowing.* Rebecca turned her face to the sky as tiny snow-flakes drifted down to melt on her cheeks. *I love snow.*

Pa cradled her carefully as they walked thru the small, quiet town. *What have I gotten myself into now?*

CHAPTER TWO

"I'M FLOATING," REBECCA TOLD PA. She felt disconnected and drunk.

He smiled down at her as she heard his feet crunch in the snow. "You'll feel more like yourself in the morning. We're taking you to the bed-and-breakfast run by a close friend. Her name is Leona. She will look after you."

"Why am I all fuzzy?"

"Can we explain that later?" he asked. "Just know that we know what's going on and you'll be fine."

She nodded. "Okay, Pa." She snuggled down into his chest.

Pa stepped up on the old wraparound porch attached to a Victorian-style home. "Our poor baby girl," he murmured.

"She is ours now," she said, softly patting his shoulder. She knocked on the door. After a few moments the door swung open.

"Good heavens, Marg, what on earth? Is the child okay?" Leona stepped aside to let Pa carry her into the first-floor guest room. He set her down carefully on the plush bed.

"Aleks inadvertently started claiming her then, abruptly left. She is still reeling from the soul merge being started then stopped." Ma pulled a soft blanket over her.

"Why on earth would Aleks do something like that? That boy has been looking to find his mate and settle down for years," Leona asked.

"That boy looked plain spooked when he bolted. Connor went after him. If I know my boy I think he's scared to hurt her. She isn't one of us," Pa said as he, Leona, and Ma left the room. Their voices grew fainter as they walked into the foyer.

"She is a tiny little thing. Well, he'll have to get over it if he wants to settle down. Everyone knows you don't go against what Fate has given you." Leona chuckled. "Leave her with me. I'll look after her."

"She doesn't know about us yet, Leona. Be careful," Pa said. Leona laughed at Pa's concern.

"Looks like someone took a real shine to this baby girl," Leona said. "Just look at that blush." Both she and Ma laughed.

Pa cleared his throat. "She's just so tiny and doesn't have anyone. I'll run back to the garage to get her things and be right back. She'll want her clothes in the morning" he mumbled.

"Come on, Aaron, we'll see her in the morning," Ma said.

Rebecca snuggled down into the soft blankets. *I'm just gonna close my eyes for a second.* Still smiling she drifted off to sleep.

"Aleks, wait up, man!" Connor sprinted after his older brother. He had never in his life seen his always-in-control brother lose it like this.

"Just leave me alone, Connor, I'm in no mood for your shit," Aleks said, walking briskly toward the sheriff's station.

"You just started claiming your mate and then walked away. What the fuck, man?" Connor demanded. "You weren't in there when she was telling us about how she got here. She has no family. I think she was brought here specifically to be your mate." Connor followed Aleks into the station.

"You saw her, Connor. What is she, like five feet tall? She's tiny! There's no way she can be my mate and live in our world. Can you see her having seven sons? Seven boys who will also be bear-shifters? If having them doesn't kill her, raising them definitely will." He threw his hat onto his desk and collapsed into his chair.

"Aleks, Rebecca is your mate. What are you going to do? Not claim her?" Connor asked, standing over him. Aleks just looked up at him then looked away.

"Please tell me you are not seriously considering letting her go? She. Is. Your. Mate. Do you know how lucky you are to have found her? I mean Fate literally hand-delivered her to you, and you're like, 'No, thank you, I'd rather jack off for the rest of my life.'" Connor watched his older brother's face. When Aleks said nothing, Connor sat in the chair across from him.

"Aleks, Fate wouldn't give her to you if you

would hurt her. You would never hurt any woman. I know that even if you don't." Connor sighed as Aleks continued to stare out the window.

"Come on, dumbass, let's go to Mojo's. It looks like you could use a drink." Connor stood.

Aleks was still scowling as he got to his feet. "She's so small," Aleks finally said.

"Yeah, bro, but they're usually the ones with the giant hearts. Come on." Connor slung an arm over his shoulder and steered his brother back out into the snow.

"You know Ma is going to kick your ass, right?" Connor chuckled. "She was really taken with Rebecca, and don't get me started on how Pa was hovering over her."

Aleks stopped then paled. "Fuck! Let's get that drink," he grumbled.

Connor laughed enjoying his brother's chagrin. Maybe Aleks needed someone like Rebecca to shake up his world.

"What in the hell was his name again? Alexander, wasn't it?" Rebecca asked the next morning at breakfast. She sat across from Leona in the kitchen. They had instantly bonded when they discovered they were both avid readers and the other one was just as quirky as themselves.

"It's Aleksander with a 'k'. It's a softer sound than the 'x'. That's what Marg said when she named him anyway. It was probably the drugs they gave her." Leona sipped her coffee.

"Why in the world did he kiss me like that and then leave? And why did I get so loopy?" Rebecca was shoveling the best pancakes she ever had in her mouth. Leona could cook like a dream.

"You want the truth?" Leona asked, pushing her hand through her blue bangs.

"Yes please, and do you have more of that maple syrup? I'm in love." Rebecca looked up and pouted.

Leona laughed. "You are going to run that family ragged, baby girl. Good for you!" Leona went to the kitchen and came back with a crock of syrup.

"He kissed you because you are his mate. You are his mate because he is a bear-shifter, and as a shifter he gets a mate picked by Fate to help him balance his man and animal." Leona sipped her coffee again.

Rebecca just stared at Leona as a thin line of maple syrup steadily fell onto her pancakes, her arm frozen as her brain processed this bit of news. She had been talking with Leona all morning, and though she was the quintessential eccentric, she seemed very down to earth. She didn't really seem like she had any screws loose.

"No shit?" she asked finally.

"No shit," Leona said.

Rebecca decided that Leona's possibly make-believe world was better than the one she was living in, and since she was on sabbatical anyway she decided to just go with it.

"So a Sherrilyn Kenyon kinda shifter or a Charlaine Harris kinda shifter?" Rebecca asked, putting the syrup down and picking up her knife and fork.

"I knew I was going to like you the second I laid

eyes on you, baby girl. To answer your question more like a mix of both. We only shift into two forms, though stronger shifters can manage partial shifts. Claws mostly. We live in family units, have extended lives and can heal quickly." Leona picked up an apple slice and popped it in her mouth.

"We? So what are you, or is that rude to ask?" Rebecca asked.

"It is considered gauche to ask, but since you're our baby girl and I know you don't have a heightened sense of smell, I'll tell you. I'm a silver fox. The Arkadions are bears. Bran McGregor and Kate Edwards lead the local wolf pack, and Liam Lewenhart leads the local lion pride. Everyone else who isn't wolf or lion is like me with neither pack nor pride. We've come to Arkadia since it's known to be a peaceful and neutral place for shifters to live without worrying about clan wars or being discovered by humans. There is a perimeter spell around the entire town and surrounding lands that protect us from humans accidentally coming upon us." She smiled at Rebecca.

"What about me? I totally found you by accident," she said, sitting back, cradling her coffee cup on her chest.

"Was it really an accident, baby girl? Think about it. You told me your car was starting to break down. Your phone's battery died. You were running out of gas. Two animals ran across your path. Do you really think that sounds natural?" Leona smoothed one hand over the tablecloth.

"No, it doesn't. If I was meant to come here, then why did he walk away? If I was meant to be his mate, why didn't he want me?" Rebecca stared down into her cup.

Leona sighed. "Because he's a man, darlin' and he is as stubborn as they come. I've seen that boy walk past an aggravated hornet's nest to stay on the sidewalk since his mama told him not to go on the street. We, that is, his parents and I, believe that he is afraid to claim you since he's afraid to hurt you."

"That is ridiculous!" Rebecca started.

Leona stood, Rebecca blinked, and she was gone. She felt an arm wrap around her throat, and she gasped.

"I apologize, baby girl, but you had to see that there is a difference." Leona took her seat as Rebecca clutched her chest.

"You scared the hell outta me, Leona!" she exclaimed, frowning fiercely.

"I know, but you needed to be a bit scared. You see, we are faster and stronger. Our bodies are heavier and bones denser. Even if Aleks were a human, a man his size would still need to be careful with you. As a shifter he is probably scared out of his mind. You are right to be upset, but please try and understand where he is coming from." Leona smiled at her softly.

Rebecca looked at the older woman and sighed.

"I see your point." She paused before continuing. "He's special to you, isn't he?" she asked.

Leona looked startled and then smiled.

"You are very perceptive, baby girl. Yes, he is. I love all of those Arkadion boys dearly. Benedict is the playboy. Connor is the happy-go-lucky one. Duncan and Emmett, the twins, are bruisers with soft hearts. Finnian is the peacekeeper, and Gavin is a brilliant yet anti-social veterinarian. I am godmother to them all. But Aleks, Aleks was always the serious one, the responsible one. Maybe in his own way he knew he would be responsible for those who not only live here in Arkadia but in all of Arkadia's sister towns." She looked lost in thought for a moment then shook her head.

"When he was just a little boy, in his quiet and serious way he always made sure to visit me and make sure I wasn't lonely. He would walk over here every day after school and do his homework at this very table while his Ma worked the diner. The other boys went out to play. Only after he finished his homework would he wave good-bye and then join them. He has a gentle heart that one. I'm so glad he has found you. He deserves to be happy." Leona smiled at Rebecca. "You're taking this really well, Rebecca, almost too well."

Rebecca just shrugged. "I have been reading nothing but paranormal books for over ten years. I love animals, and I felt the connection pulling me to him. I have no family and no home. I come here, and not only is he the most gorgeous man I have ever seen in my life, he is also my mate destined and created for me by Fate. He comes with a large and loving family and a shifter town as a home. The only possible problem is that he can turn into a huge apex predator that can defend and protect me. What exactly is the downside?" she asked.

Leona threw her head back and laughed. "Well, if you put it that way." She was still laughing as she stood. She picked up the breakfast plates. Rebecca stood and grabbed the silverware.

"Hey, Leona, were you supposed to tell me all this?" Rebecca asked, following her hostess to the sink.

"Well, usually your mate would be the one to explain everything to you. But considering he has his head up his ass and you're living in an all-shifter town, I thought it might be best to tell you up front. Why?" Leona rinsed the plates before placing them in the dishwasher.

"He's the sheriff, right? I could have sworn he was in a uniform last night," Rebecca asked, smiling.

"Baby girl, what are you up to?" Leona asked curiously.

"I'm going to go visit a bear," she said with a grin.

Aleks trudged back to the sheriff's station from the diner, his head pounding with one of the worst hangovers of his life. He didn't know whether it was from the volume of alcohol he consumed or the lingering side effects from stopping the soul merge. Both Ma and Pa had laid into him the second he stepped into the diner for breakfast. His ears were still be ringing. He knew walking away from Rebecca would be bad, but he hadn't known what effects a partial soul merge would have on his mate. He battled with himself. He wanted to go to her and make sure she was okay. But he also wanted to keep his distance.

He sat down laying his head back on his chair. Maybe he should just take the day off, go back to bed, and pretend he dreamt the past twenty-four hours. With his eyes closed, he remembered how she smelt. Like honeysuckle and vanilla. His dick hardened and his mouth began to water. He remembered her soft, dark curls and bright violet eyes. He had never seen eyes like hers before. She was small but her mouth felt like heaven. He could imagine her warm soft lips wrapped around his cock. He shifted in his chair trying to adjust his rapidly shrinking pants. He imagined her on her knees looking up at him, saying his name.

"Aleks."

"Yeah, baby," he replied.

"I'd like to report a hit and run," a soft feminine voice said. Aleks's eyes flew open and there, standing before him, her head tilted to one side, was his mate. She looked down at his crotch, her eyes widened, and a red blush worked its way up her neck to her cheeks finally tinting the tips of her ears.

He scooted so that his legs were under his desk obscuring his lower half. Her words sunk in, he stood up and flew around the desk. He lifted her up placing her down in his chair.

"God! Are you okay? Where were you hit? Why aren't you at the clinic? You need to go to the clinic!" He stood unsure whether he should pick her up. What if she had a neck injury? Why in the hell was she up and walking around?

"Yes, you see, last night I was minding my business at the diner, trying to eat dinner. When this man came in, kissed me until I was unconscious, then left. That has to be at least a felony, right?" she asked, her eyes blinking up at him innocently.

Aleks felt relief pour through him at her words.

She was okay. She hadn't been hit by a car. He sat down in the chair across from her and leaned forward his elbows on his knees and his eyes on the floor.

"I'm extremely sorry about that. It wasn't like me at all. I was hoping we could forget about it," he said.

"Did you mistake me for someone else?" she asked, frowning.

"Uh... no," he answered, looking down at his hands.

"It was an amazing kiss. It seems a shame to forget it. No. I don't think I will. In fact, I think I want another one," she said shyly.

His head snapped up and she was standing in front of him. Even with him seated in the chair and her standing he was almost taller than she was. She stepped between his knees, leaned down, and pressed her lips to his.

Her scent filled his nostrils, and his hands automatically came up as if with a mind of their own to cup her firm ass. She moaned and leaned into him. He stood pulling her up into his arms before wrapping her legs around his waist. He could smell her arousal and knew if he dipped his hands into her jeans that her panties would be soaked through. He needed her. He needed her more than he needed his next breath.

Holding her up with one hand, he wiped his desk clear with the other then laid her down on the dark walnut desktop. Without taking his lips from hers, he cupped her mound through her jeans. She moaned loudly and ground her hips against him, needing more friction. He made quick work of her jean buttons and pulled the denim past her rounded hips and down her thighs where they pooled at her knees. He ran his fingers through her folds to find them dripping wet. He pulled back from their kiss and sucked his fingers into his mouth.

"You taste like the sweetest honey. I can't wait to have more," he said, smiling.

She groaned and tried to open her legs wider for him but was trapped by her jeans. He smiled wickedly.

He pulled her sweater and tee shirt up, exposing a simple white lace bra. He smiled and lowered his lips to the hint of pink he saw flashing at him through the lace. When his mouth found his prize, she screamed out and bucked against his hand. He ran his fingers over her clit before plunging one finger into her silken channel. She cried out as her body began to shake. He continued to pull on her breast and grind his hand between her legs until her hips stopped moving against him and her breathing slowed. He felt his bear calm down as he breathed in her scent. Unable to control it, their souls came closer together.

"Wow," she said simply, smiling up at him drowsily.

"Ohhh Aleks! I come with coffee and pastries to help your hangover." A voice called from the door. Connor appeared in the doorway. "Shit! Sorry! I didn't see anything!" He dropped the bag of pastries on the floor and took off at a run.

Despite the awkward position she found herself in, Rebecca started to giggle. Aleks looked down at her dancing eyes and he smiled. He helped her sit up and right her clothes.

"What about you? Your, um, you know?" she said, pointing at his crotch. His cock felt like it was about to rip through his pants.

"Honey, if my pants come off, you'll find yourself in a more compromising position than the one my brother found you in." He smiled at her.

Her eyes widened and her mouth formed a small 'O'. Then, in a flash, the look of innocence turned to one of pure mischievousness.

"Really?" she asked.

Aleks just shook his head. Maybe he wouldn't hurt her, because she was well on her way to killing him.

She sat down and watched him pick up his desk items, putting them back in certain positions on his desk. "Now what?" she asked. " I don't really go around having orgasms on men's desks."

He growled low and swung around. "No man gets to do that but me," he growled out.

Her eyes met his squarely. "So we're dating?" she asked.

"No," he said shortly. He ran a hand through his hair. His best intentions were shot to hell. He immediately felt guilty for what just happened.

"So we're not dating?" she asked hesitantly.

"No," he said again. He may have slipped up, but he needed to keep the bigger picture in mind. He needed to keep her safe even if it was from himself.

She wrapped her arms around her body. He hated to see what was clearly a defensive position.

He took a deep breath and concentrated on what as important, keeping his tiny mate safe and in one piece. He turned his back to her so she wouldn't see him waver.

"Okay then, um, goodbye I guess." She stood and walked out the door.

He'd live a lifetime of hell to keep her alive.

This had not turned out the way she imagined. She thought as her mate, he would realize how much they belonged together and he would get down on his knees and pledge his love. She shook her head. Okay, maybe not that, but she thought they would at least get together. She hadn't expected his out-and-out rejection.

When she turned back, he still stood beside his desk, not moving, his back to her. She walked out of the building and was wiping at her eyes when she ran into Connor, who was waiting outside the front door. His eyes were kind, and she knew he heard what Aleks said.

He nodded and went into the station. She followed silently, knowing it was wrong to eavesdrop, but wanting to hear what Aleks would say.

"Dude, what the fuck?" she heard Connor demand, only slightly muffled by the cracked door.

"I don't need her. I need a shifter female who can give me cubs. I can't be mated to a human," Aleks said harshly.

"If you don't grab her, someone else will, someone like Liam, who can appreciate a good-looking, sweet, and adorable woman like Rebecca!" Connor yelled.

She covered her mouth with her hand and ran

back to Leona's. Being alone was a thousand times better than meeting your soul mate and having him rip your heart out.

She kept her head down as she made her way back to the familiar bed and breakfast. She hurried up the wooden steps of the porch and rushed inside accidentally slamming the door into the wall in her hurry to get inside.

"What in the world?" Leona asked, walking into the foyer from the front room. She took one look at her and shook her head. "Come here baby girl." Rebecca flew into her open arms. "He hates me!" she wailed as Leona steered her to the comfortable den. Only after she was settled into the sofa with a hot cup of tea did Rebecca tell the understanding older shifter what happened.

Leona ran her hand over Rebecca's hair.

"Give him time, baby girl. He didn't mean that he didn't want you. He always thought that his mate would be a shifter," Leona explained softly.

"What about me? I had to adapt to knowing shifters existed and then finding out I was mated to one. I think I'm doing really well." She sniffled into her sleeve.

Leona reached over to the side table, grabbed a tissue and handed it to her.

"I think there is more to his story than any of us knows. But I have a feeling that before all is said and done, you will know why. Now, instead of moping around here, why don't you head to the diner? Everyone will still be there for their breakfast, their second breakfast, or early lunch. You can meet some more of the townspeople." She patted Rebecca's shoulder.

"Okay, though I don't feel like being social," she said, sitting up.

"Go have fun, baby girl. Remember you aren't mated yet, and there are some fine-looking men in this town. There is nothing wrong with looking and flirting. Ask me how I know," Leona said with a wink.

Rebecca smiled slowly.

"You're right. Be back later." She got up, headed toward the door before turning back to give Leona a hug.

"Thanks," she said simply.

"Anytime, baby girl. Now go have fun."

CHAPTER THREE

ALEKS PACED BACK AND FORTH in his office. How did she know that flea-bitten no-good alley cat? She had only been in town overnight. Liam wouldn't say no to his sweet Rebecca. That man couldn't keep his dick in his pants. Rebecca wouldn't know what he was like. He growled and paced some more.

"If the growling is because of me, I'm sorry for bursting in on you earlier, but in my defense the door was unlocked," Connor said from the doorway.

"How does Rebecca know Liam?" Aleks asked.

Connor frowned. "They met last night at the diner. He said something about putting a bell around her neck like a kitten."

He saw Connor jump as he released rage filled roar. He felt his canines drop and hands extend into claws as his brother's face noticeably whitened. When Aleks moved toward the door, Connor intercepted him, wrapping his arms around his brother's waist. "Aleks, control yourself! You're losing your shit here. If Ma sees you walking around town like this, she'll skin you alive." Connor was hanging on, and even at his height and weight Aleks dragged him toward the door in the effort to get his hands on Liam.

"She's mine! Mine!" Aleks growled.

"I thought you decided to let her go," Connor reminded him, still holding on.

"I did!" Aleks said, his breathing slowing down. Connor waited until his claws had retracted before letting him go.

"Then what's the problem?" Connor asked as they both sat down.

"My bear wants her bad. I can feel him clawing at me to go to her, to put my mark on her and claim her," Aleks said, balling his hands into fists.

"Then I ask again, what's the problem?"

"The fucking problem is I have seen firsthand what one of our kind can do to a human. Derek and I..." He swallowed hard.

"Your partner from when you were living in Raleigh?" Connor asked.

Aleks nodded. "He and I were called in for a reported domestic violence call. It was routed to us since the residence belonged to a wolf-shifter and we worked in the shifter-only unit. When we got there the male opened the door and just walked us to the back room. She... she..." Aleks ran his hands over his face. "She was broken. Her right arm had been dislocated and nearly torn from the socket. Her pelvis had been crushed, and she had obviously torn during sex. Her legs were a bloody mess. He just stood there so completely out of it. My partner cuffed him and got him in the car. I waited for forensics then we left. He's in jail, but she's dead. I can't get her out of my mind. She was bigger and taller than Rebecca. If that could happen to her with a wolf, what damage could I do to tiny Rebecca as a bear?" Aleks stared down at his desk.

"Did you tell Ma or Pa about this?" Connor asked.

"No, I couldn't think about it anymore," Aleks said.

"That's why you left Raleigh and came home, isn't it?" Connor asked.

Aleks nodded. "I figured there were no humans here to get hurt like that," Aleks said.

"I only have one question. Were they mates?" Connor asked.

"What the hell difference does that make?" Aleks demanded. "She didn't deserve to die that way, whether they were mates or not," he said.

"Were they mates?" Connor repeated.

"I don't think so," Aleks said.

"I can tell you that they weren't based on what you said. What male looks down at his mate and sees that kind of damage and has the cognitive ability to call the cops? If they had been mates you would have been called in due to the sound of gunshots fired, from him blowing his head off. No male could live with the knowledge that he brutalized his female and killed her. He would be chasing her soul into the hereafter begging for forgiveness," Connor said heatedly.

"What's your point?" Aleks asked.

"My point is this. Picture Rebecca. She's smiling at you, right. She grabs your arm to pull you along then she trips and you reach out to right her." Connor paused. Aleks nodded.

"Now picture her arm bruised at your hand." Connor said this flatly. Aleks's head snapped up.

"How do you feel?" Connor asked.

"Like someone has kicked me in the balls, like I'm going to be sick, and I want to cry like a baby," Aleks told his brother, knowing he would never admit this to anyone outside his family.

"Aleks, don't you see? That's from thinking of a bruise. You are her mate. You were designed and born to love and care for this one female. It's in you, right down to your DNA to keep her safe. Do you really think that Fate would put you with a female whose presence caused you both pain?" Connor asked softly.

"You really don't think I'll hurt her," Aleks said.

"No" Connor said.

Aleks started to smile. "I can claim her," he announced.

Connor nodded.

"I can claim her," he repeated excitedly.

Connor laughed "Yes sir, you can."

Aleks stood. "I'm going to claim her. Where is she?"

Connor pulled out his cell phone and his fingers flew as he sent a text. "I'm checking with Benedict, he's helping out at the diner today." A second later he grimaced at the response.

"She's at the diner talking with Liam." Connor quickly moved out of his brother's way.

Aleks rushed out the door. "I'll kill that son of a bitch if he touches her."

"Liam! Put me down!" Rebecca giggled as Liam lifted her up his hands under her arms and swung her around over his head.

"I can't help it. You are so small it's like lifting a feather." He wiggled her around.

"You are courting death," Kate said as she started her fourth waffle.

"I'm not afraid of that grouch," Liam said, tossing her up then catching her. She squealed.

"Aleks will maul you like the bear he is, my friend," Bran said, his arm casually draped around Kate's shoulders. Rebecca found out that since neither of them could cook, they were both frequent patrons of the diner. Bran said he had to make sure his mate was well fed.

"Shush!" Kate said, looking at Rebecca. Bran's eyes widened. Rebecca smiled, figuring out why they looked so guilty.

"It's okay, I know you're shifters," Rebecca said as Liam swung her around. He paused.

"You're okay with us being shifters?" Ma asked from behind the counter.

"I kinda thought Leona was a bit crazy when she told me," Rebecca started.

"She is one of a kind." Ma chuckled.

Rebecca smiled and nodded. Liam had settled her on his lap.

"But no, I don't mind. I mean you're not all that different than me." She fought the urge to roll her eyes as nearly every patron hid a smile at her declaration.

"Aleks is lucky to have you," Bran said.

Rebecca looked down at her twisting hands. "He doesn't want me. He said we weren't dating and that he didn't want a human. He wanted a shifter female to give him cubs. So I don't think he has me at all," she whispered softly.

Kate growled in her throat. "Ma, what is that boy's problem?"

Ma shook her head. "He's working through some things. Don't worry, Rebecca darling. He will come around. I didn't raise stupid boys. He'll realize how special you are."

"Y'all are the kindest people I have ever met. I feel real lucky to have come here. Almost like finding lost family," Rebecca said, smiling at Kate.

Kate sniffled. Bran cuddled her close. "I can't help it. She's just so sweet," Kate said.

"She's so sweet I could eat her up," Liam said, nuzzling her neck, trying to lighten the mood.

A low ominous growl filled the diner. Everyone turned to see an extremely pissed-off bear standing in the doorway.

Rebecca, remembering Aleks's words just that morning, wrapped her arms around Liam's neck. She felt him tense for just a second then he relaxed. She would have to find a way to make this up to him. He was willing to go along with whatever she did and was rapidly becoming best-friend material.

"Get your goddamn hands off my mate!" Aleks roared.

"Aleks, language!" Ma yelled.

Rebecca shook her head. "You don't want me, remember. I'm not good enough for you. You want a shifter for a mate, not a lowly human." Her eyes stung, and she turned her face into Liam's shoulder.

She heard Liam hiss at Aleks over her head.

"Cat, you have five seconds to hand over my mate before I rip you apart," Aleks said, stalking forward. He was brought up short as Rebecca turned and met his eyes. She could practically see his rage drain away when faced with her pain.

She hopped off of Liam's lap and walked over to Aleks. Instinctively Aleks took a step backward.

"No. You. Will. Not!" She repeatedly poked her finger into his abdomen where she could reach him. "You had your chance. I literally gave myself to you on a silver platter, and you threw me away. Go find the shifter wife that you want."

"Baby, please listen. I..." Aleks started.

"No, I won't listen. You were so afraid to hurt me physically you never stopped to think if you were hurting me any other way. You ripped my heart out, Aleks. Maybe it wouldn't hurt so bad if I didn't know we were meant to be together. If you were just a random guy I liked who rejected me I could just walk away, but you're not. You're my soul mate, and you don't want me. How can anyone love me if you don't?" she said, her voice breaking.

Aleks stared down in horror, realization slowly dawning on his face. His eyes showed he now knew the depth of the pain he caused her, and it had nothing to do with bruises or broken bones.

He stepped forward to reach for her and was brought up short when he saw Liam standing directly behind her.

Liam wrapped an arm around Rebecca's shoulders and steered her toward the door. "Come on, kitten, I can show you around town," he said and

Rebecca nodded.

Aleks growled. Liam turned his head,"Back off, asshole!"

"Aleksander Aaron Arkadion, get your ass in my office now!" Ma roared before turning and heading into the kitchen.

Aleks's head hung down as he made his way behind the counter to go and speak to his mother and Alpha.

Rebecca couldn't find it in her to think about his pain, her own was threatening to overwhelm her. Unable to take the looks of pity from the diner patrons she let Liam lead her out the door.

Once they were outside Rebecca lost all sense of composure and started to sob uncontrollably. She almost laughed at the frantic expression on Liam's face as he looked around for someone who could help him. Seeing no one nearby, he scooped her up, walked around to the side of the diner and put her back on her feet so she could have her breakdown in private.

"I really like him, Liam, I really do!" she cried.

"I know, kitten. I know things are hard right now. I can't believe I'm about to say this, but, he's really a good guy. He and I have been competing since I beat him in a foot race when we were five. I know him probably better than anyone except his brothers. Now listen, kitten, I know that he hasn't handled this well," he said, and she snorted. He smiled at her unladylike gesture. "But what no one in town knows is that the reason he came back to Arkadia was because he worked a real bad homicide case in Raleigh where a human was killed by her shifter lover during sex. The only reason I know is because I hired a private detective to find out what happened. When Aleks got back to town, he had lost weight, wouldn't eat, and snapped at everyone. I had to provoke him into a fist fight before he started to feel better. Of course I won," he said, smiling down at Rebecca. She felt herself smile through tears.

"No wonder he is having a hard time accepting me for a mate," she said.

Liam kissed her forehead. "I would love to keep you for myself, kitten, but I know you'll be happier with your grumpy-ass bear," he said jokingly. "So no more waterworks okay? You're breaking this poor lion's heart."

"He is grumpy, isn't he?" she said and smiled.

"Of course he is, he's a bear. Now, how about I show you around our fair town? We have a killer ice cream parlor, and don't get me started on Nic's frappes." He wagged his eyebrows.

"How come you're not mated?" she asked. He was gorgeous, witty, charming, and considerate. Everything a woman could want.

He smiled sadly. "Because Fate has yet to give me one."

They were about to walk away when they heard a tiny mewl. Rebecca swung back to the alley. She went to step forward, but Liam pushed in front of her. Together they walked to the back of the alley. Rebecca gasped and Liam turned quickly. She bent down and picked up a small, bedraggled cat. She hugged it close.

"Look at the poor thing! It must be freezing out here," she said.

Liam eyeballed the small animal. "What are you

going to do with it?" he asked.

"Take care of it, of course! It doesn't have any family or a home."

He smiled, and reached forward to pet the small creature. He looked surprised him when it turned its head into his hand and purred loudly. Rebecca lifted it up and checked near the back legs.

"It's a boy cat!" she announced happily and nuzzled it. "Okay, his name will be..." She trailed off, looking the little face over as it stared up at her.

"Sebastian," Liam supplied.

"That was quick, what made you think of Sebastian for a name?" she asked.

"I don't know, it just sort of popped in my head. Doesn't he look like a Sebastian?" he asked.

"Yes, he does. Do you hear that, little one? Your name is Sebastian. Do you think he would like some ice cream?" she asked.

"I think he'd love some." Liam laughed.

"Let's go!" Rebecca bounced out of the alley then realized she didn't know where she was going and turned to face Liam. He laughed and walked up, looping his arm in hers.

"Onward to ice cream," he said turning the corner with her.

Rebecca kept nuzzling the small cat in her arms. The poor thing was still purring madly, happy to be held. She smiled up at Liam when he opened the door to the ice cream shop. Carefully she set Sebastian down as they walked over to the large display case.

She watched Sebastian stand up on his hind legs and peered into the case, mesmerized by the smells.

"I think he wants some ice cream. See, his paw is

pointing to Butter Pecan," Rebecca said, watching her cat.

"I'll be damned, it is." Liam replied.

"Hey, Liam, who's your friend?" a light male voice asked.

When Rebecca looked up, she saw one of the most beautiful men she had ever laid eyes on. He wasn't handsome. He was almost feminine in his beauty with bright blue eyes and soft lips. His shoulder-length blond hair framed his faces in waves. She couldn't help smiling at him.

"You are so pretty," she said without thinking. He looked at her, blinked then laughed.

"Thank you. I have to say so far I've only heard that said behind my back. It's refreshing to have someone tell me to my face and not as an insult." He chuckled.

"Why would anyone say that as an insult? You make me feel bad for not being a great artist or sculptor or something. It's like..." She looked up, trying to think of the words to explain herself. "It's like your beauty is wasted on my eyeballs," she said after a moment or two.

The man blinked again then turned to Liam.

"She's serious, isn't she?" he asked. Liam nodded.

"Rebecca is very special. It seems she accepts everyone for who they are and likes them despite themselves. She will make a very good Alpha Mother," he said.

The man paled then looked at Rebecca. "My apologies, Alpha, I didn't know." He looked down.

Rebecca turned and looked up at Liam. "This is a shifter thingie, isn't it? And what is 'Alpha Mother'?" she asked.

Liam sighed. "Ashby here isn't a pack leader like most of the town's residents that you've met so far. He is showing you deference out of respect to your rank once your mating with Aleks is complete. After mating you will become 'heir to the throne.' When Ma retires you will take over as the town matriarch as Aleks will take over as patriarch. The Arkadions have always run Arkadia. They are trusted to be neutral in shifter disputes. Historically, the Alpha couple always have seven sons. The eldest son and mate takes over when the current leaders retire. It's been that way since the town was first established. Prior to that I believe that the family ruled in Europe. It is said that the Arkadions are descended from Arcas, the son of Callisto, the first bear-shifter. To me they are just a bunch of grouchy bears though," Liam said, shrugging in a very cat-like manner.

Ashby eyed Rebecca as she started to sway.

"She's going down," he said simply.

"Shit!" Liam wrapped his arm around her waist as her knees gave out.

"Seven boys. They all have seven boys. Seven. Boys." She kept repeating this over and over.

"Liam, I think you broke her." Ashby came around the counter waving his dishtowel to fan her.

"She'll be fine," he said in a way that sounded like he was trying to convince himself rather than Ashby.

"Right, kitten? You don't want your good friend Liam torn to itty-bitty bits because I scrambled your brain." Liam lightly tapped her cheek.

"Yeah I'm okay, yeah, wow, seven." She looked

at Ashby.

"I'd like a quadruple death by chocolate mocha fudge sundae with caramel, *Oreo* crumbles, and brownies please. Oh and Sebastian would like one scoop of Butter Pecan," she said, moving to sit in the chair across from Liam.

Ashby, seeing her need for chocolate, put his preternatural speed to good use and whipped her up the chocolate concoction that would help her face her destiny. He set the dessert in front of her before putting a tiny bowl on the floor for Sebastian. He walked around the table to sit across from them.

They watched her eat spoonful after spoonful. When she was done she leaned back her stomach distended.

"Oh my God, I bet sex isn't as good as that," she said after she scrapped the last of her ice cream off the bowl. Ashby giggled and Liam groaned.

"That bastard gets all the luck. Untouched? You are almost too perfect." He shook his head. She stuck her tongue out at him.

"Okay, kitten, where to next?" Liam asked as he paid for the ice cream. Rebecca went to fuss at him for paying, but the look he gave her silenced her protest. He was easily the most elegant gentleman she'd ever met.

"I'm dead, don't ask me," Rebecca said, almost lying in her chair patting her stomach. She turned to look at Ashby. "Where should I go next?"

Ashby looked surprised that she was asking his opinion. "If I had that much ice cream, I would want some coffee I think, to settle my stomach. My best friend Nicholas runs the Grind, it's the coffee shop across the street," he said shyly.

Rebecca got up and faced Liam. Sebastian purred at her feet. "Coffee please," she said. He nodded and offered his arm again. They were almost to the door when she whirled back to Ashby.

"Okay, I know it's the worst possible manners, but I have to know. What do you shift into?" she asked, looking at him expectantly. Liam slapped his forehead with his palm.

Ashby looked surprised but quickly recovered. "It's okay since you look like you won't make fun of me and Liam knows already." He closed his eyes, then disappeared as he shrunk down out of sight behind the ice cream case.

Liam looked thoughtful then said, "Ashby is very reticent about revealing his animal. He must really like you." A tiny animal appeared from around the tall counter. Rebecca inhaled then quickly scooped him up.

"You are without a doubt the most adorable animal I have ever seen!" She turned to Liam. "I want him," she said, snuggling the small animal's white fur. He had large eyes and larger ears. Liam laughed. She rubbed her cheek against the top of his head then kissed it.

"Sweetie, he's not a pet, he's a Fennec, a rare type of fox-shifter," he explained.

Rebecca put him down and he ran back around the counter. He shifted back and pulled his clothes on, obscured by the ice cream case. Once dressed, he came back around to stand with them.

"You're the first person to not look down at my animal," Ashby said, smiling shyly. "Most of the shifters in town are predator animals, lions, bears or wolves. So us smaller animals are usually thought of as weak." He didn't meet Liam's gaze.

Liam just nodded. "He's right. Food chain mentality and all," Liam explained.

"Well, that's just silly since you're all human." She picked up Sebastian, who purred.

Liam and Ashby just stared at her.

"What?" she asked, looking back at them.

Ashby just smiled widely. "You're right, Liam, she is special. I look forward to her being *my* Alpha Mother," Ashby said, inclining his head.

Liam's eyes widened at Ashby's choice of words and pushed Rebecca forward. "To acknowledge him and establish your rank over him, lean forward and lightly touch your lips to his neck," Liam explained.

"B-b-but I'm not over anyone," Rebecca stuttered.

"You will be. Ashby is giving you his fealty and his respect, but he is also asking for your protection," he explained.

"I'm doing this because you're my friend and I would take care of you anyway," Rebecca said leaning forward to touch her lips to the side of his neck. He let out a blissful sigh. Rebecca felt a distinct shift in her heart as she felt tiny strands bind them together. She was no longer alone. "He's mine," she realized, touching her chest. She knew that this moment had changed her. She had finally found a place to call home.

Movement by the door had them both turning to see a seedy looking man moving away from the entrance. Liam's eyes narrowed. "Damn hyenas." He looked down at her then shook his head. "Come on, kitten, let's get you some coffee then go check on your car. I'm interested in seeing your 'toy' car, as Pa puts it." He steered her toward the door.

"Bye bye, Ashby, see ya later," she said, waving. Ashby smiled wide and through their bond she felt that for the first time since moving to Arkadia, Ashby felt like he could really call the shifter town home.

"Sit down son," Ma said when they reached her office, located in the back of the diner, past the kitchen. Aleks sat with his elbows on his knees and his face in his hands. She looked over and the lecture she was about to give him seemed to die on her lips.

"Do you finally want to tell me what happened in Raleigh?" she asked softly.

He lifted his head to meet her eyes. "It was a bad case, Ma. The poor girl was torn up horribly. I had nightmares for months. I just couldn't shake it." He looked down and stared at the floor.

She walked over and firmly cuffed him in the back of the head. He looked up, shocked. She paused, then cuffed him again.

"Ma!" he exclaimed. When he brought his head back up she had tears in her eyes.

"What have your Pa and I done that made you feel like you couldn't come to us after a trauma like that?" she asked.

"Nothing! Ma, you and Pa are the best parents

a guy could ask for. I felt like if I talked about it when I was here it would follow me. I should have been able to handle that on my own," he said. He ducked when she reached out to cuff him again.

She put her hands on her hips. "You have a family that loves you and would fight and die to keep you safe and happy! Do you know how much it hurt us to see you suffering and we couldn't do anything about it? It felt like you didn't trust us to help," she said.

"It wasn't like that," he said, shaking his head then he sighed. "You're mad at me, and I've probably ruined any chance I have with Rebecca. Maybe she would be better off with Liam," he said. His head jerked forward as her hand came down on the back it.

"Ma!" He rubbed the back of his head.

"Don't be dramatic, Aleksander. Of course you are clearly the better choice, all my sons are. You just need to show her, not tell her, that you really care and want her." She smiled slyly. "Isn't your Pa working on her car now at his garage?"

He nodded absently then stopped and looked up smiling. "Love you, Ma," he said, standing and giving her a huge hug.

"Love you too, baby boy. Now, go get your mate. I can't wait to finally have a daughter," she said, rubbing her hands together. Aleks laughed quickening his pace as he left to go help his Pa with his mate's car.

All the way to the garage he thought of ways he could make it up to Rebecca. Flowers? A gift? He was still strategizing when he walked through the open bay doors.

His Pa was staring down at a little toy.

"Hey Pa," he said walking over to his father.

"Did you talk to your Ma?"

"Yes, Sir," Aleks replied.

"Do you want to talk about it?" Pa asked as he stared down.

"No, Sir," Aleks said, also staring down.

"Aleks, your mate is tiny," Pa said, rubbing his hand over his chin.

"Yes, Sir, she is." Aleks frowned and gulped nervously, he wondered if he was going to get a lecture about sex and mating. He hoped not. That would be awkward.

"She fits in this car," Pa said, pointing down.

"This is a real car? Wait! This is her car?" Aleks, exclaimed, looking down at the tiny vehicle in front of him. "I thought you were building something to enter into that innovative engineering contest you go to every year," Aleks said, frowning at the death trap before him.

"Yes, I watched her drive up to the bay doors and get out. She even had room for her luggage too," Pa said, scratching his head. "Now, I can work on it, but I can't get in to change gears." He looked at his son who stood taller than him by an inch.

"I could get her a new car. Like an Excursion or Hummer," Aleks said.

Pa shook his head. "Her car is one of the only things that survived the house fire that claimed her father's life," he replied.

Aleks felt frustrated. It seemed like everyone knew more about his mate than he did. Of course he had only spoken three or four sentences to her. He sighed.

"It will be okay, son. Your mother didn't talk to me the entire time I held her prisoner on the mountain before we were mated," Pa said.

"Uh-huh," Aleks nodded then he froze as the words sunk in. "Wait, what?" Aleks asked, feeling stunned.

Pa gave a lazy shrug. "She was so stubborn. She fought our mating and refused to speak to me. So I just bundled her up one night, put her in the trunk of my car, and drove her out to your grandfather's hunting cabin. You were conceived in that cabin." Pa smiled as he reminisced.

"I thought you said she didn't talk to you the entire time?" Aleks questioned.

"Son, as old as you are, I'm sure you know by now that talking has little to do with cubs getting made. At the end of the second week she finally said, 'Okay, I'll keep you.'" Pa laughed.

"I think if I tried that with Rebecca she might kill me in my sleep. She was really pissed at me," he said, eyeing the car from a new angle.

"I could tell right off she had fire. She'll be a perfect mate for you, boy. Don't know why it took you so long to see it. You're stubborn though, just like your Ma, once you get something in your head you need a crowbar to get it out." Pa just shook his head.

"I want to fix her car, but I don't want her driving it. The thought of her hurt gives me a heart attack. And I want to learn everything about her. I'm tired of hearing others tell me about her and not know it myself. She's my mate, dammit! I should know about her car and her family." Aleks sighed. "It seems like I only know one thing about her." He turned to his Pa "Did you know she has the smile of an angel?"

Pa nodded and then motioned with his head to the door.

"Do now," he said grinning broadly.

Aleks turned to see his mate standing before him clutching a bedraggled cat. She had tears in her eyes.

"Did you really mean all that?" Rebecca asked. Aleks nodded, afraid to move forward. He would let her make the first move. She bent to set the cat down. It immediately twined around Liam's legs as the man leaned against the open bay door. She walked over and stood before him.

"We could have dinner together," she said, looking up at him. He just nodded like a bobblehead. He was surprised when she crooked her finger at him to lower his head. He leaned down. She smiled and lightly kissed him on the lips. He jerked up, then smiled widely.

"See you tonight, bear. Oh, and I'm keeping my car," she said before waving at his father. "Bye, Pa."

"Bye, baby girl," Pa replied.

Aleks growled at Liam, who gave him a shit-eating grin before wiggling his fingers at him behind Rebecca's back as they walked away.

"Pa, how long before you get the car fixed?" he asked rubbing his chin.

"A couple years," Pa said, smiling.

"Sounds about right to me," Aleks said before he headed back to the station to pick up his car. He was on a mission to make arrangements for the most perfect date night in the history of all date nights.

CHAPTER FOUR

"HE REALLY CARES ABOUT ME," she said for the third time. She still felt amazed from hearing Aleks' confession in the garage.

Liam just nodded. "Of course he does, you're his mate," Liam said as they walked.

"I heard what he said to Connor. He said he wanted a shifter mate," she said quietly.

"He wanted a shifter mate because to him it was safer. We can't hurt shifter females the way we can human ones," he explained.

"Liam, did I take you away from your job today? What would you normally be doing?" she asked. They finally turned off of Main Street. She could see the clothing store down on the right.

"I work from home, investments and stock management. At this point in my life I really don't have to work much. I mostly keep my raggle-taggle group of lions from eating each other. We're a backward bunch in that we're a group of males. Normally in the wild it's a group of lionesses with only one male. But females are so rare." His voiced drifted off.

"I know Fate has someone just for you, Liam. You're too awesome not to have a mate," Rebecca said. Liam smiled.

"I hope you're right, because if something doesn't change, lion shifters will become extinct." He sounded sad. Rebecca hugged him.

"Come on, I need to find something to wear. I only have jeans and sweaters. I want something pretty for tonight." Rebecca giggled as he rolled his eyes.

"How did I get stuck clothes shopping?" Liam asked.

"Because you're my friend," Rebecca said simply, looking up at him.

"You sure know how to hit a guy in the gut," Liam said, ruffling her hair.

"Hey!" she said, batting at his hand.

"Come on, kitten, time to get your date outfit," he said, grinning.

"I can't choose!" Rebecca yelled, dramatically falling back onto Liam's leather couch. She had no idea which dress to choose. After shopping, Liam had spirited her off to the pride house and she was currently surrounded by male lion shifters.

"This one is simply divine, you have to wear it." The dark-haired Adonis held up the black slip dress that she had initially chose. It was simple, yet extremely sexy. He laid it to one side to rummage around in her make-up bag that she had picked up from Leona's on the way to Liam's.

"Rian, are you blind? This one is clearly the dress to wear. It's elegant and shows a more refined side." The auburn-haired man held up a modest pink chiffon dress that screamed vintage elegance.

Rebecca sighed. That had been the crux of her internal argument as well. She went back and forth between the two at the store, so in order to preserve his sanity, Liam had bought her both despite her protests about being an independent woman, then marched her to his car so that he could enlist his pride's assistance in helping to get her ready.

"Damian, that one is a little too good. She will never get him to claim her if she wears it. Maybe later, after they've been together a bit she could bring it out when she wants to tease him," Rian explained, now looking through the bag for the matching shoes.

"You may have a point. She does want him to be out of his mind with lust. The claiming is always better that way." Damian agreed.

"Hair up or down?" Rian asked, holding up a pair of three inch black heels.

"Definitely a half-'n'-half. Half up to show sophistication and half down to look tousled." Damian nodded his approval at her shoes.

Rebecca watched in rapt fascination as the two men plotted her outfit as if they were commanders on a battlefield. When she voiced that observation, all the men stopped and laughed.

"Honey, it is a battle, and we're going to make sure you are the victor. Now what is your objective for the night?" Rian asked pulling her over to sit between himself and Damian. Rebecca looked up in search of Liam. When she met his eyes, he smiled then nodded.

"They may appear to be crazy, but these men represent the most reliable group when it comes to dating advice," Liam said.

"Except you forgot me!" Kate exclaimed from the foyer shutting the door behind her.

"Kate! Katie Belle! Kate!" The group exploded in welcomes.

"How dare you sequester her away planning a date night and not call me, Liam. I am hurt! I had to hear about this pre-dating party from Leona, after I went to the bed and breakfast looking for you after I heard about the dating shopping spree from Miranda who was gloating that you were shopping in her store," Kate said with a mock growl, then unable to keep up the angry façade collapsed into laughter on the sofa across from Rebecca.

"Besides, I come with the best components. Rich red wine, rich dark chocolate, and rich vanilla cheesecake," she said, grinning when the men erupted into cheers.

Rebecca laughed. "My objective is to make him regret rejecting me, make him pant after me, and make him realize I could be a good mate even though I'm not special like y'all," she said.

Kate frowned and sat up. "You are special, Rebecca," she said. Liam made his way to the couch, moving Rian over to sit next to her.

Rebecca shook her head. "Not like y'all. You are freaking awesome. You can shift into these amazing animals. I'm just a boring old human," she said sighing.

"I bet wherever you worked you were well

liked," Kate said.

Rebecca nodded. "A lot of people are well liked at their jobs," she said.

"I bet you knew everyone on your block where you lived," Liam continued.

"A lot of neighborhoods are close," she replied.

"I bet a lot of people smile at you for no reason," Damian added.

Rebecca looked at them in confusion. "But that's normal stuff," she refuted. Everyone smiled at her.

"One, maybe two of those, but all of them? Kitten, you have a way of bringing people together. Ma is a wonderful Alpha Mother because we know that she will protect us and she runs a tight ship. But you, kitten, will be a perfect Alpha Mother because you will love everyone in this town, and for the first time, make this feel like a real community. Not bears, and wolves or lions, but families and friends. That is why Ashby has already given you his allegiance. He sees in you what I do. Someone who will not just protect us, but love us and help us grow," Liam said softly.

"He's right, baby girl. Ma has our loyalty and respect, but I could see us giving you our love. Even though we haven't known each other very long I know you'll put the people of this town first. I honestly believe that Fate delivered you to us when we needed you the most. We may be a safe haven for shifters, but it doesn't feel like home. You could do that for us." She handed Rebecca a slice of cheesecake.

"I don't think I can do all that," she said, suddenly feeling very small.

"That's the thing, kitten, you already are. Kate

and I are normally at each other's throats, bickering, you know the whole cat, dog thing. But we instinctively put that aside to help you. Aleks may be the one enforcing the laws, but you will be the heart. Our leader. Kate was right when she said we need you now more than ever. We need someone who can unite not just the town but also different species outside of Arkadia." Liam reached over and grabbed her fork, stealing a bite of cheesecake.

"Is it too late to join the party?" a soft voice asked timidly from the foyer.

Everyone looked up to see two men standing in the foyer waiting for permission to come in.

"Ashby!" Rebecca launched off of the sofa. She ran over and wrapped her arms around him, giving him a hug. "The guys are helping me pick my outfit for tonight. I have a date with Aleks," she announced, smiling.

"We know. Nicholas and I were closing down the coffee shop when Miranda came in to tell us how Liam had you out shopping. I'm afraid you are the only source of gossip right now." Ashby looked over at the room full of lions nervously.

"We brought coffee," Nicholas said shyly. Rebecca met Nicholas when Liam took her to The Grind. She was just as taken with him as she was with Ashby. Where Ashby was blond and ethereal, Nicholas felt like an old friend. He had brown shaggy curls that fell carelessly perfect about his face. He had sinfully creamy skin and warm, rich brown eyes.

"Thank god!" Rebecca stood on tip toes to kiss Nicholas on the cheek. He blushed furiously.

Everyone sat down and started to talk at once.

Rebecca noticed that Ashby and Nicholas stayed close by her side, and Kate and Liam seemed to take the roles of hall monitors. Rebecca smiled as Ashby and Nicholas seemed to open up.

"It's like you guys never hung out before," she said and everyone looked at her.

"We haven't," Ashby said, looking into his coffee cup.

"If you weren't here, we wouldn't feel safe enough to surround ourselves with predators. But we know you would keep us safe," Nicholas said.

Rebecca swallowed hard. She didn't feel comfortable with the level of absolute trust they all seemed to have in her.

"We wouldn't hurt you," Damian said, pouting.

"You wouldn't intend to, but we have seen the aggressive natures of predator animals take over. It's never pretty," Ashby said.

"Now you know they won't hurt you, right? Because we're all friends now," Rebecca said assuredly.

Everyone just stared at her.

"Right?" she asked.

"You wouldn't hurt Ashby or Nicholas because you all are amazing men and wouldn't hurt anyone that was smaller than you. I trust you all," she beamed at the room.

"Not everyone believes as you do. We get judged because we're male lions, but we're really not aggressive, or we would never be able to live together like this. Normally a pride is a group of females and one or two males. We're a group of misfit males," Rian said, wrapping an arm around Damian.

"We are left out of town decisions and are picked on because we're small," Nicholas said, mirroring Rian's action by wrapping an arm around Ashby.

"Everyone thinks I have a say in the pack, but we have a faction that is close to going rogue and who doesn't listen to me. I know that Bran would object to me discussing pack business but it's true. None of us seem to know each other or what is really going on in this town because we've never just sat down and talked to one another," Kate said, hugging a pillow to her chest.

"You knew you could come to me, we may bicker but you had to know I'd be there for you," Liam said, moving to sit on the sofa. "I would have helped."

"You would have, but would your pride have helped?" she said and saw the conflicted looks on the faces of the pride members around her.

"But all that is in the past, because from now on we're going to help one another, just like you're helping me for my date," Rebecca said happily. When her words sunk in, she looked at everyone in panic. "My date! It's in less than two hours and I haven't even showered!" She stood up and started moving toward the stairs but didn't know where a shower was. She still didn't even know which dress she was going to wear. She started to hyperventilate.

Immediately everyone sprang into action. Kate grabbed her by the hand and started to drag her toward the stairs.

"Liam, get the guys to decide on a dress. Ashby, Nic, I'll call you in a few minutes to do her hair and makeup. Someone call Aleks so he knows to pick her up here. Uh, Liam, not to be funny, but it should be you. And don't torture him too much when you call." Kate got Rebecca up the stairs. When she looked over the bannister Liam stood in the middle of the room.

Liam looked around at the men staring at him.

"Well, you heard her," he said and everyone started to move.

"Aleks, hey, buddy," Liam said lazily after the grouchy bear answered his phone.

"Hey, asshole," Aleks replied sounding distracted.

"I just wanted to call and let you know that you'll be picking up Rebecca at my house for your date." Liam waited. Three, two, one and... he held the phone away from his ear at the roar.

"What the hell is she doing at your house?" Aleks growled.

Liam smiled. He was making this too easy. "Well at the moment her luscious little self is in my shower and wait, yes, I smell coconuts. She's bathing." He once again held the phone away from his ear at the roar, as everyone stopped what they were doing to listen.

"If you so much as lay one finger on her, cat, I will rip you apart," Aleks threatened.

"What was that, Rebecca? You need help getting into your dress? Don't worry, kitten, I'm coming. Sorry, Aleks, have to run. Toodles." He stayed on the line long enough for one last roar to come through before disconnecting the line. He turned around whistling and saw everyone staring. "What?" he asked.

"Aleks Arkadion is going to kill you," Ashby said, white as a sheet.

"No he isn't. If he didn't kill me for wrecking his Charger, he won't kill me now," he said, sitting down on the sofa. He reached over and grabbed a magazine and started to flip through the pages.

"That was you?" Rian asked, his eyes wide.

Liam just chuckled.

"Aleks. Can't. Breathe," Liam gasped as Aleks squeezed his hands around Liam's throat. Aleks was surprised at the lack of interference he was getting from the pride. They just shrugged their shoulders.

"Ashby told him you were going to kill him," Rian said shrugging.

"Where is Ashby?" Aleks asked, his hands still choking Liam.

"He's upstairs finishing Rebecca's hair. Nicholas did her makeup. She put in a lot of effort for you, bear, so you better not fuck this up," Rian said, crossing his arms over his chest.

Aleks raised an eyebrow. The pride seemed to be more protective of Rebecca than their Alpha, whom he had pinned to the wall.

"Oh for God's sake, Aleks, let him go! You'll upset Rebecca and ruin your evening before it begins," Kate said, coming down the stairs. Aleks immediately dropped Liam.

"Kate, why are you here?" he asked.

"How could I miss the opportunity for actual girl time? We don't have much of that in the pack," she said, swiping a piece of chocolate.

Aleks opened his mouth to say something when he heard a door open and Rebecca appeared at the top of the stairs. Her scent hit his nose, and he felt his chest constrict. How could he have possibly thought he could stay away from her? She gracefully made her way down the stairs, with Nicholas and Ashby following behind her. Once she stood before him he got the full effect of the dress. It had tiny spaghetti straps that seemed to accentuate her delicate shoulders. The black dress made her creamy skin glow, but it was the lone slit up one side was nearly his undoing. He didn't realize he was growling until Liam hit him in the ribs. Rebecca just blushed and smiled up at him.

"Ready?" he asked, holding out a slightly trembling hand. She nodded and moved forward, placing her hand in his.

"Goodnight, everyone, thank you, for everything," she said, smiling at the room.

"Have her back before midnight, young man," Liam said, standing in front of the pair his hand on his hips.

"Out of the way, cat," Aleks muttered. Rebecca stepped forward and gave Liam a hug.

Aleks growled. She ignored him.

"Goodnight, Liam." She kissed his cheek. Aleks growled again.

"I'm serious though, if you don't want to go back to the bed-and-breakfast we made up a guest room for you. That's where Sebastian has been hiding. I let Leona know you may be staying here," Liam said, smiling down at her.

"Watch him for me?" she asked. Liam nodded.

"Who's Sebastian?" Aleks asked.

Rebecca waved. "Goodnight, everyone." She started walking toward the door.

"Who's Sebastian?" Aleks asked again, wrapping his arm around her waist.

Once outside he stopped in front of her to open the car door. Blushing furiously she sat down and he closed the door. He quickly made his way around the car and got in.

He pulled away from the house. "Seriously, who is Sebastian?" Aleks asked when they turned onto the main highway heading away from town. Their reservation was for eight, which gave them plenty of time to get there.

"How was your day?" she asked, smiling up at him. He sighed then smiled back at her.

"Better after having seen you in the afternoon," he said.

"Did you catch any criminals?" she asked.

He laughed. "No, mostly I help to mediate disputes between families. Today I followed up with Bran's men about checking the perimeter. Everyone in town knows not to hunt near the road. We believe there may be hyenas close by," he said.

"Hyenas don't follow the laws put forth by the council, right?" Rebecca asked.

Aleks looked at her in surprise. "Exactly, did Liam tell you that?"

"Yes, he has been explaining a lot to me, Leona too. This is all completely outside my realm of knowledge," she said.

Aleks frowned. "I should have been the one to explain these things to you. I'm sorry," he said, meeting her gaze.

Her eyes widened. "Let's not think about that right now. Let's pretend this is a typical first date with no drama," she said.

"I can do that." He pointed to the radio. "Plug in your phone and play your favorite music. I want to learn everything about you."

He knew he had finally done something right when her eyes lit up. She plugged in her phone and soon Aleks was tapping his fingers on the steering wheel to music he had never heard before. Some of it wasn't even in English.

All too soon they arrived at the restaurant. "I kinda wish we could keep driving," he admitted.

"Me too," she said shyly.

They were seated right away. Aleks smiled at the way Rebecca's wide eyes took everything in. "This place is fancy," she whispered.

He nodded. "You deserve nothing less than the best." He leaned forward and took her tiny hand in his. Aleks frowned, her small hand was so cold.

He immediately got up and wrapped his jacket around her shoulders. He then motioned to the waiter. "Can you please turn up the heat in here? My lady is freezing." He indicated to Rebecca, who was swimming in his suit jacket. The waiter smiled at her then nodded at Aleks.

"Of course, sir." He walked away to make the adjustment.

"Why did you do that?" she asked as he sat back down. He couldn't help but smile. She looked absolutely adorable being swallowed up by his jacket. He liked that his scent was covering her now.

"Do what?" he asked.

"Give me your coat and asked them to turn up the heat," she said.

"Because you were cold," he said, confused.

"So just like that you did something about it?" she asked, tilting her head.

"Yes, you are my mate. It bothers me on every level to know that you are cold and uncomfortable," he said simply.

She just smiled softly then nodded.

The rest of the dinner went smoothly. Aleks learned that his mate was intelligent and kind. She was fierce when she talked about something she was passionate about. He found himself learning new things about some of the townspeople from her. She observed everything through fresh unbiased eyes.

When the waiter came up and let them know it was closing time, Aleks was surprised. Time had flown by so quickly during their magical dinner. There were never any awkward silences, and it seemed as if they went from strangers to old friends somewhere between the appetizer and dessert.

Aleks walked her to the car and noticed the sad look in her eyes. He pulled her against him and raised her face to his with his hand.

"Hey, what's wrong? Didn't you enjoy dinner?" he asked softly. She nodded.

"Then what's wrong? If I can fix it I will," he said.

"I'm afraid that when we go back this spell will be broken and you won't want me anymore," she said as tears started to spill down her cheeks.

"Oh God, baby, no, please don't cry. I don't care if it takes me the rest of my life to prove to you that I need you, I will. Things between us will only get better and better. I'm not fighting our mating anymore," he said and used his thumbs to wipe away her tears.

"You promise?" she asked, placing her small hands on his large ones as he framed her face.

"I promise," he said then leaned in slowly, giving her time to back away. He gently brought their lips together. He felt her hands tighten on his as she leaned forward kissing him back. He gave a low growl and deepened their kiss.

"Do you think the bear will share his human?" a voice asked.

Aleks looked up and swept Rebecca behind him.

"Back off, hyena, you know the laws," Aleks said, baring his descended canines.

"We're not in Arkadia, bear! You don't rule out here," another voice said from behind Rebecca. Before Aleks could move, they grabbed her and were pulling her toward a car. The hyena that had been in front of him now stood with another between him and his mate.

"Aleks!" she screamed.

He could feel his bear straining to break free. He let out a roar and charged the two hyenas blocking his way. He brought his arm up and raked his claws across their chests sending them to the ground. He ran after his mate and quickly caught up to her. He reached out and flung the hyena dragging his mate into the building.

"His hands are shifted!" one yelled.

"Of course my hands have shifted, I am an Arkadion. We're one of the original shifter families. A partial shift is child's play to me." He turned and started backing Rebecca up against their car. He could feel her trembling against his back.

"This isn't over, bear. She's worth too much, we need her." The hyena that had been flung stood wiping his mouth.

"You threaten my mate and I will personally kill each of you with my bare hands," Aleks said.

The hyenas cackled nervously, all three shifted and ran into the brush.

"Get in the car!" Aleks ordered. Rebecca scrambled to open the door. Only when she was safely inside did he race around and jump in the driver's seat. He watched as her trembling hands tried and failed to buckle her seat belt. Gently he took the belt from her hands and clicked it for her.

"It will be okay, baby, they will never touch you," he said and kissed her forehead.

Her entire body shook beside him. Enraged, he took out his phone. Within seconds he had Liam, his parents, and Bran conferenced in and on speaker.

"I need you to send an escort to meet us and get us into town safely. I am taking no chances with my mate," Aleks said.

"Connor, Rian, Damian, Emmett, and Duncan have already left. Kate is coordinating with them on a separate line," Ma said calmly.

"Rian and Damian were most adamant to be the ones to guard your mate," Pa added.

"They ju–just want t–t–to hear how th–the date went. They are s–s–so nosy," Rebecca said, her teeth chattering.

"Aleks, turn up the heat, it sounds like she is going into shock." A familiar voice advised.

Aleks looked over and saw that Rebecca was still shaking and started cursing as he jacked the heat in the cabin. He recognized the tenor voice as Dr. Claybourne. He was glad his Ma called him in. He wanted to make sure Rebecca was okay. How dare those hyenas threaten his mate! He cursed again under his breath.

"Aleks, language!" Ma said and Aleks smiled at the familiarity of it.

"Yes, Ma," he said and pushed the gas pedal down further.

A little before the halfway mark, which proved to Aleks how fast his brothers must have been driving, they met up with their escort. Two trucks did hairpin turns and flanked his car. Aleks let out a breath, feeling better now that his brothers were with him.

"The others are here. We should be home in less than thirty minutes," Aleks said.

"Bring her straight to the diner. I want to lay eyes on the both of you," Ma ordered.

"Ok, Ma, love you."

"Love you too, baby boy, hurry home," she said and he hung up the phone.

"I'm sorry our date was ruined," he said softly.

"It wasn't ruined. You were willing to fight and kill for me. That shows me how you feel more than any words can say." She grabbed his hand and held on tight.

"I would do anything for you," he said and she smiled.

CHAPTER FIVE

"SHE'S FINE, ALEKS, NO HARM done," Dr. Claybourne said, stepping back from Rebecca. Aleks breathed a sigh of relief.

"Repeat what he said again," Ma asked.

"I don't know. It was something about Rebecca being worth too much," Aleks said, running his hands through his hair, causing it to stick up in different directions. Rebecca realized what would look messy on another man made him look like he just got out of bed. Yum.

"He said, 'This isn't over, bear. She's worth too much, we need her.' Then they left," Rebecca said, blowing on her hot chocolate.

"Okay, that was creepy," Connor said.

She looked around. "What was creepy?"

"When you repeated what he said, you kinda sounded like him, babe," Aleks said.

"Oh, yeah, I do that. I have an eidetic memory, sort of," she said, sipping her drink.

"Really?" Aleks asked, sounding surprised.

She knew having a photographic memory that could also recall sensory impressions was quite rare. There were times she hated it. "Yeah, it sucks sometimes. When I hear something that makes me sad, it stays with me a long time and I can recall it with perfect clarity, like when the police came in to tell me my father died. I remember exactly what he said and how he sounded. Or like the other day when you were talking to Connor and you..." She trailed off.

Aleks stood and picked her up before placing her in his lap and wrapping his arms around her. He nuzzled the back of her neck and she giggled. Everyone smiled at them.

"How soon can we close our borders to them?" Aleks asked.

"We can't," Ma said softly.

"Why the hell not?" Aleks roared.

"Because we can't prove that they were acting with their clan's approval. If we close the borders to them they could bring charges against us for not remaining neutral. It could lead to the dismantling of not only this town but Arkadia's sister towns as well." Ma explained.

"That is bullshit!" Rian exclaimed. Heads nodded.

"But that's the reality we have to deal with," Ma said.

"Come on, baby, let's get out of here," Aleks said.

She shot a look to Liam and then Rian and Damian. Rian was the first one to realize what was wrong.

"You can't take her away, Aleks. She is coming home with us so we can hear all about your date," he said, winking. Aleks began to frown. Damian chimed in.

"That's right, she owes us a story." Damian stepped up and scooped Rebecca out of Alek's arms. Aleks began to growl. Rebecca turned and faced him.

"I'm not saying no, just not tonight. Please understand," she asked, looking down at Aleks, pleading with her eyes.

He sighed. "Take all the time you need baby, I'll always be waiting."

"Don't forget to pick up your luggage from the bed and breakfast. You will want a change of clothes for the morning," Leona reminded her.

"Thank you, Leona."

"My door is always open to you, baby girl," Leona said.

Aleks stretched. "I suppose one night won't be too bad, but they have to feed me in the morning. I'll be over for breakfast," he said, grinning evilly at Liam, who rolled his eyes.

"I also want to cook you dinner tomorrow to make up for the way tonight's date ended. Would that be okay?" he asked.

She nodded, smiling, and then leaned forward from Damian's arms and kissed him.

"Okay, no smooching in my arms, it's weird," Damian said, laughing.

Aleks turned to his brothers. "Emmett, you take first watch, and Connor, you can take second. I'll take third watch and then stay for breakfast. I want her watched at all times until we can close the borders to those damn hyenas," he said.

His brothers nodded. "We got this, Aleks," Emmett said. Both brothers pounded fists with Aleks. Emmett grabbed the thermos of coffee his ma had prepared and handed it to Connor.

Liam scowled at Aleks. "We can guard her just fine."

"Yeah!" Rian and Damian said echoing their Alpha.

Aleks ignored them. "See you in the morning baby."

"Goodnight," she said, waving as Damian huffed then carried her out of the diner.

Once everyone had piled into the car Damian leaned forward. "Okay, do you want to explain why we rescued you from what would have been a primal claiming? He was totally amped up from defending you. It would have been hot!" Damian demanded, waving his hands beside her in the backseat.

"I don't know," she admitted watching buildings go by as she stared out the window.

They drove for a few short blocks before stopping at Leona's. Rian hopped from the car and went inside.

She began to giggle when he ran from the door, dramatically flew off the porch her suitcase under one arm and jumped into the vehicle like it was a getaway car.

"Drive! Drive!" he shouted making them all laugh.

Once on the road she looked over to Damian. "I think he has accepted that he has a mate, and I think he has even accepted and is okay with a human being his mate. But I want him to want me, Rebecca, as a mate. Does that make sense?" she asked, turning to look at Damian.

"I understand what you mean, darling, but here's

a little inside information. For shifters, when we meet our mate, that is it. Aleks may have had reservations about you being his mate since his protective instincts were in overdrive and he didn't want to hurt you, but he and his bear know you are it for him," Damian said.

"Tonight was magical. I felt like we really got to know each other, but he doesn't know everything about me. How can he already accept me as a person?" she asked.

"Rebecca, for shifters your mate is your everything. Before you, Aleks may have only dated tall, Nordic blondes who were built like linebackers. But now he is only attracted to tiny, dark-haired humans. Everything in him wants, no, needs everything that makes you, you. You have found the one person in this entire world that will love you and crave you, just the way you are, because just the way you are makes you perfect for him," Rian explained from the passenger seat.

"Just like that?" she asked. All three men nodded.

"In our world finding your mate is like winning the lottery. Our whole culture teaches us to cater to our mates, because we know how much of a blessing it is. Mates always, always come first," Liam said.

"Tall, Nordic blondes?" she asked, and all three groaned.

"You would pick up on that one single sentence." Damian playfully smacked her on the arm. She laughed.

"So enough of the self doubt, tell us everything! I want details, woman. Aleks has been the most eligible bachelor and most sought-after shifter in town. He's always so intense." Rian turned around and stared at her in rapt attention. She smiled.

"Ahhhh! Look at that smile. I know something happened, tell all, woman!" Rian exclaimed.

"Well, he took me to this perfect little restaurant outside of town," she began before launching into the story of dinner, his passionate kisses, and him defending her against the hyenas. She had Damian shaking his head and Rian pretending to swoon in the front seat. She laughed at their antics. In her heart she started to believe that maybe Aleks actually wanted her for her.

CHAPTER SIX

"**W**HAT DO YOU MEAN SHE isn't here?" Aleks demanded when he knocked on Liam's door the next morning.

"She left about a half an hour ago to head to town to ask Ma about getting a job," Rian explained from the foyer.

Aleks stared at him for a second then turned around and went back to his car. He grumbled under his breath the entire way back to town. He was going to throttle Liam for leaving. He knew Liam just didn't want to make him breakfast. Thinking of food had his stomach growling. Maybe going to the diner wasn't such a bad idea. He could find Rebecca, talk her out of getting a job, eat a huge breakfast, beg for forgiveness, then take her home and claim her before spending the day fucking her silly. He nodded. Yup. That sounded like a perfect idea.

"What do you mean she isn't here?" Aleks asked his Ma. He looked around the diner half expecting her to pop up from one of the booths.

"She left with Liam to go ask your Pa about the

library. It's been closed for a while and she's real interested in getting it back in order. When I told her that she would have carte blanche if she was interested in getting the library updated, she lit up like a Christmas tree. Did you know she has a Master of Science in Library Science and another Master of Science in Computer Science? I think that girl is an authentic genius," Ma said, handing Kate a plate filled with pancakes. Aleks stared at his Ma.

"So she went to the garage?" he asked, and his Ma nodded. Shaking his head, Aleks gave Kate's pancakes a wistful glance before turning around to head to his Pa's garage.

"What do you mean she isn't here?" He stood dumbfounded at his Pa's garage. How fast was his mate moving?

"After I gave the okay and found the keys to the library she and Liam took off to go get her 'Orgasmic Frappe' I think she called it," Pa said from under Emmett's truck. Aleks frowned. That would explain why he didn't see her, if she took Congress Avenue down to Nic's place. Growling and now starving, he left to go to the coffee shop.

"What the hell do you mean she isn't here!" Aleks exclaimed. Most of the patrons moved closer to the door. Nic went white as a sheet.

"Sir, Alpha Aleks, sir, she and Liam already left to go to the diner to speak with your Ma." Nic gulped when he saw that Aleks's canines.

"Goddamn cat! I know he is doing this on purpose!" Aleks marched toward the door as people practically jumped out of his way.

"What do you mean she isn't here!" Aleks roared

before reaching for Liam, intending to choke the life out of him. Liam jumped behind Kate and Bran, who were having a hard time not laughing.

"You knew I would be over this morning. You knew I would be looking for her. I know you have been taking her the long way around town. You had to have caught my scent!" Aleks bellowed.

"Aleks, she..." Liam began.

"I want to see my mate! Where is she?" Aleks demanded.

"Aleks, she..." Liam began again and was cut off as he tried to avoid Aleks's hands.

"I'm right behind you, you grumpy-ass bear. Now sit down. You're being too loud," Rebecca said, standing in the middle of the diner with her hands on her hips.

Aleks immediately quieted down and walked over to her, placing his hands on her shoulders, and rubbed his chin over her head. Liam grinned wickedly.

"What I was trying to say was that she wasn't here because she was in the bathroom," Liam said, taking his seat at the counter.

"Aleks, quit causing a ruckus! Rebecca, your breakfast is ready," Ma said, placing another plate next to Liam's at the counter. Aleks steered Rebecca toward the counter and sat her down, kissing her forehead. She grinned up at him. He reached over, grabbed Liam's plate, sat down on the other side of Rebecca and began to inhale the food.

"Hey!" Liam exclaimed and Ma rolled her eyes. She headed back to the kitchen to grab a plate for Liam and probably a second plate for him.

Rebecca turned to Aleks, excitement written all

over her face. "I have a job! Your Ma found out I used to be a librarian before I moved and recommended that I look at your library, which hasn't been open in years. I was shocked when I found out about that. I mean how can you not have new books to read? Anyway, she then said I should check with your Pa to get the library keys. He said he thought I would be the perfect person to get it back to its former glory and gave me the keys. Then we went to see Nic because it's morning and I needed my frappe and then we came here. I meant to call you, but I left my phone on the charger at Liam's. What did you do this morning?" she asked seemingly all in one breath.

He blinked then smiled. He was beginning to love her little rambles. When she looked up at him, she looked so sweet he couldn't stay mad. Besides, it wasn't her fault. It was the damn cat!

"I was looking for you," he said simply and pushed the empty plate aside as his Ma came back with a breakfast for Liam and a second plate for him. He smiled at his Ma and then dug into his second breakfast.

"A word of warning for you, baby girl. All my boys except for Connor are grumpy bears first thing in the morning. For bears usually morning sex and a huge breakfast will make them more human and less grouchy," Ma said, pouring more coffee for Rebecca. Liam and Aleks's mouths dropped and Kate began to crack up behind them.

Rebecca nodded thoughtfully. "I'll have to remember that. 'Fuck him then feed him,' bear instruction number one," Rebecca said with a grin as she leaned down and dropped a slice of bacon on the floor for Sebastian, who started purring madly.

"That may just be shifter instructions, Rebecca, because I do the same for Bran," Kate said between bouts of laughter, wiping the tears off her cheeks. Bran turned scarlet.

"Rebecca, language," Ma said, grinning before winking at Kate.

"Becca!" Aleks said, shocked at her language. She turned and looked at him questioningly, her head tilted to one side. Liam dropped his head to his forearms, he was laughing so hard.

"You have no idea what you're in for." Liam laughed. "I've spent nearly the past twenty-four hours with Rebecca. I have a feeling she isn't as meek as everyone thinks she is. There is a definite spunkiness hidden there dying to come out."

"Liam and I are headed to the library. There is so much to do!" Rebecca said excitedly.

Aleks nodded. "Becca, how about after your work at the library I'll pick you up and I'll cook you that dinner I owe you," he said casually. Inside he was desperate to get some alone time with her.

"Sounds perfect," she said, smiling.

Feeling devilish, Aleks grinned as he pushed the second empty plate away. He stood up and swung her around on her bar stool until she faced him. He leaned forward and kissed her gently. When he felt her relax against him he ran his tongue along her lips until she opened for him and he caressed her tongue with his as he nibbled at her lips. When she gave a tiny whimper, he pulled back and kissed her forehead.

"Have a fun day at the library, Becca." He turned to Liam. "Watch over her, asshole," he said before walking out the door. From her half-vacant expression, he knew he had done well. Whistling, he started toward the sheriff's station.

"Goddamn bear!" He grinned as he heard Rebecca's frustrated voice carry over the traffic.

CHAPTER SEVEN

WHEN REBECCA AND LIAM LEFT the
diner, he was still poking fun at her.

"You better watch out, Rebecca. It seems like all he has to do is kiss you to scramble your brains. All that higher education goes right out the window," he said, grinning.

"Har, har, very funny. I can't help it, that man knows how to kiss." She sighed happily.

"I'm just glad to see you happy, short stuff," Liam said, reaching down to ruffle her hair.

"Hey! Stop doing that!" she said, giggling.

She turned laughing and ran into another man.

"I'm sorry," she said automatically. Looking up, she quickly stepped back. It was the same man who tried to grab her at the restaurant. The man looked down at her and growled before he pushed her against the brick wall of the theater. She felt the air whoosh out of her lungs a second before her head slammed against the brick building.

"Hello again, little human." The voice growled. The man moved to grab her. Rebecca tried to scoot away and inhaled as sharp pains radiated from her breastbone.

Liam threw back his head and let out a roar that nearly blew out her eardrums. She had only heard him hiss and growl up to this point, but that was nothing compared to the soul-shaking male lion roar. People exited stores and buildings to see what was going on. Rebecca slid down the side of the theater and collapsed on the sidewalk. Sebastian stood in front of her with his back arched, hissing up at the man.

Ma exited the diner as Pa came running up behind Liam from the garage. When they both saw Rebecca on the ground, they let out enraged roars of their own. All seven of the Arkadion sons appeared from every corner of the town including Aleks.

Liam moved toward the man. "I'm so glad you came out to play, hyena," he said with a thick gravelly voice as he circled the stranger. The hyena looked around panicked. He obviously hadn't expected Liam to get involved.

Pa moved forward and carefully picked Rebecca up. She let out a whimper. The hyena's response to Liam was drowned out by Aleks' roar as he shifted to his bear form and knocked the man down. He stood over him and roared again. He swiped the hyena's face and chest with his six-inch bear claws.

Ma walked up and said, "Aleks, let him up. You need to tend to your mate." She turned her attention to the snarling hyena. Aleks padded over to where Pa stood with Rebecca. He got on his hind legs and pressed a large wet black nose into her neck. Hands shaking, she ran her small hand over the fur on his face.

"Your kind has been warned. Arkadia is open to all shifters as long as you do no harm to any of the residents. You have harmed one of our people. From this point on your clan is legally banned from Arkadia and all of her sister cities. There is nothing the council can do," Ma said, facing down the man.

"She is not one of our kind. She is only a human," he spat out, his lank blond hair hanging in sticky, bloody clumps around his face.

"That girl is my daughter." She growled. "She will bear my grandchildren, who will one day be the leaders of Arkadia. She will be the Alpha Mother and rule beside Aleks. She belongs here more than you do." She then turned to Liam.

"Liam, will you escort this animal out of town?" she asked.

"Mother Arkadion, it would be a pleasure and an honor," he said, grabbing the man by the hair, and literally started dragging him down the street, making sure to hit every hard object in their path.

Ma rushed over to where Pa cradled Rebecca. Aleks had shifted back to his human form and stood next to his father peering down at Rebecca.

"Aleks, you're naked," Rebecca said swallowing hard, she was beginning to feel sick.

Connor came running from his trip back to the diner. He handed Aleks a pair of sweats and a zip hoodie. Aleks smiled and nodded his thanks to Connor.

"Not for long, sweetheart. What happened?" He quickly dressed as his mother started checking Rebecca over.

"The hyena shoved me against the wall. I think

he was trying to stun me, then he went to grab me, but Liam stepped in. He looked surprised that Liam was willing to defend me," she said, breathing shallowly.

Rebecca moved in Pa's arms and gasped as the sharp pains stole her breath.

"Ma!" Aleks exclaimed urgently.

"Quickly, Aaron, we need to get her to the clinic," she said, pushing Aleks forward.

Aleks stayed by her side as his father walked quickly but carefully across the street. Aleks was relieved to see Dr. Claybourne was waiting for them at the door.

"I heard the roars and figured someone would be heading my way. Who is my patient?" he asked, directing them towards the examination table.

"Maddox, it's Rebecca. She was the one you looked at last night. A hyena shifter threw her against the brick wall of the theater." Ma relayed the information to the doctor.

"Marg, I need for you to get everyone into the waiting room, including your son." He looked up where Aleks held Rebecca's hand.

"No!" Aleks argued.

"Do as the doctor says, Aleks. The quicker he can tend her, the better," Ma said.

"I'll be okay, Aleks. Don't forget our date. You're supposed to cook me dinner," Rebecca said, smiling weakly.

He nodded running his hand over her hair. "You just concentrate on getting better."

"Okay," she whispered. In truth she didn't want him to leave, but she had a feeling Aleks might accidentally maul Dr. Claybourne during her exam.

"I'll be just outside," he called as the room emptied.

That alone warmed her heart. It had been a long time since someone was there for her, it felt good.

Ma led him out of the examination room. Snarling at everyone, Aleks walked toward the waiting room. More than anything, he wanted to stay by his mate's side. He exhaled slowly, now that the threat had passed he felt drained. He collapsed into one of the waiting room chairs.

"She'll be okay, right, Ma?" he asked, desperately needing to hear her say yes. If Ma said Rebecca would be okay, then he knew she would be.

Ma looked at him and smiled sadly. Pa took the seat next to him and placed a hand on his shoulder. Each of his six brothers took up places in the waiting room like sentinels.

Liam walked in thirty minutes later, his knuckles bloody. When Aleks saw the state of his hands, he stood up and hugged Liam. Liam patted his back and they both sat down.

"How is she? She hit that wall hard," Liam asked quietly.

Aleks growled. "Doc hasn't come out yet. She could barely move when we brought her in. She is so damn fragile." His voice broke.

"She's a fighter though, you'll see." Liam sat back so they sat shoulder to shoulder. He turned to him in a low voice. "That bastard will be lucky to reach his car by sundown. I tried to break every bone in his body. Their clan may cause issues later." He rubbed his knuckles.

"Let them come," Bran said from the doorway. Kate rushed in and hugged Ma.

"No one comes into our town and hurts our girl," Kate said firmly. "You have the pack's support," she said. Bran nodded.

"You have the pride's support as well," Liam added. Rian and Damian had walked in behind Kate and Bran. Rian held a purring Sebastian. "I called some pride members in to help patrol the town."

"You have us too," Leona said, walking in last with Ashby and Nicholas. Ashby looked pale.

"Marg, hun, I didn't think you'd mind, I put up a 'Closed' sign at the diner," Leona said, hugging her friend.

Aleks stared at all the people in the waiting room.

"She's only been here a couple days. How...?" His voice trailed off as he looked at everyone.

"She's special," Ashby said simply.

"She's easy to love," Kate said and smiled at Ashby.

Aleks looked over as the doc walked out. "How is she, Doc?" he asked, jumping to his feet.

"She's in a lot of pain, but thankfully nothing is broken," Doc said, facing the room full of people.

"She won't die?"

The doctor smiled kindly. "No, Aleks, she will be just fine, just sore for the next couple days. Her breastbone is bruised, and it will make it painful for her to breathe tonight. I gave her something to help her sleep."

"I need to speak to her. I never got the chance

to beg for forgiveness or to make her dinner," he said softly.

The doctor chuckled. Aleks's head snapped up.

"What could possibly be funny?" he demanded. The doctor looked at the angry bear-shifter his lips twitching.

"After I gave her medicine to relax her, all she kept saying was, 'I have a date with my goddamn grumpy-ass bear. I want to see my grumpy-ass bear'," The doc laughed at Aleks' expression.

"She said 'my' grumpy-ass bear?" Aleks asked. The doc nodded. Ma and Pa were smiling.

Aleks smiled widely. "I'm her grumpy-ass bear," he said loudly, causing his brothers to snort and laugh.

"Shit, I've been telling you that you were grumpy for years. You never listened to me," Liam said. Aleks punched his shoulder.

"Can I see her?" Aleks asked. The doc nodded.

"Just for a few minutes, she needs to rest," he said, and Aleks quickly stepped past him and through the swinging doors. He made his way to Rebecca's bedside.

"Hey, baby, I heard you were calling me your grumpy-ass bear," he said lightly brushing his fingers over her forehead.

"You are my bear. Don't forget our date. You owe me a home-cooked meal," she said drowsily.

Aleks swallowed against the lump in his throat. "I won't forget, but you have to get better first. Doc says you need to rest and you'll be better in no time. Liam is here. So is Kate and Bran and Leona and Ashby and Nicholas," he said, naming all of her new friends.

"I love Ashby. He is so cute I want to snuggle him," she said, smiling. Aleks' mouth dropped and he stared down at his mate horrified.

"I love his white fur. He's so soft," she continued. His heart began to beat again when he realized she meant his animal form.

"I'll tell him you said so."

"Take care of my Sebastian, my baby," she said and dozed off.

He leaned forward and kissed her forehead then went back to the waiting room.

"Ashby, she said that you are cute and wants to snuggle you," he said, frowning down at the smaller man. Ashby turned ashen as he stared up at the large shifter.

"Sir, I..." he started. Aleks held up his hand. "She also said that she loved your fur and it was soft."

Ashby blushed and Nicholas laughed.

He looked at the people in the room, his face darkening.

"Who in the hell is Sebastian?" he demanded.

CHAPTER EIGHT

"**H**OW DID I GET STUCK with the cat?" Liam asked.

Aleks laughed. "Because the cat clearly likes you more than me," he replied.

"Because you already have a litter box at home." Connor smirked.

"We're lion shifters, you asshole, we don't use litter boxes!" Liam growled out.

The cat in question rubbed his face against Liam's chin and purred loudly. Connor and Aleks turned away to hide their smiles.

Connor and Liam were the last to leave the clinic. Ma, Bran, and Kate had already headed to the diner to discuss the possibility of hyena confrontations. Leona, Ashby, and Nicholas left earlier to return to their own places and Rian and Damian decided to patrol the town hoping to find some hyenas to play with.

"I'm heading home. Aleks, tell Rebecca I'll bring Sebastian by when she is feeling better." Liam put two fingers to his temple, gave a small salute, and walked out.

Connor turned to Aleks. "I'm going to the diner to help out with the dinner rush then I'll come back here to help keep an eye on things. Liam is right, the hyenas will be causing trouble. Dr. Claybourne rolled out two bear-sized cots for us," Connor said, pointing to where one cot was set up next to Rebecca and the other in the waiting room.

"Thanks, Connor, I really appreciate you coming back," Aleks said.

"No problem, I'll bring back some to-go boxes when I return for the night, it should tide us over till breakfast." He waved then jogged out the door.

Aleks walked to where Rebecca lay sleeping and looked at her face. With her eyes closed she looked different. He realized how much her large eyes dominated her face and how much of her heart you could see in her eyes. He sat down, took her small hand in his, and started telling her about himself.

When Rebecca woke up later that evening, Aleks was speaking softly. She loved hearing his deep voice tell her stories of his childhood. She almost laughed out loud a few times when he was telling her stories about him and his brothers growing up. They sounded like they were still close and possibly still getting into trouble, especially the twins Duncan and Emmett.

When he fell silent, she shifted her legs and

opened her eyes, pretending to wake up. He was sitting in the chair next to her, staring at her with a smile on his face. She smiled back.

"Are you hungry?" he asked, pointing to a couple of to-go boxes on her nightstand.

"I'm starved. What do we have?" she asked, looking around for the remote to her bed. Aleks lifted the remote and brought the bed up to a sitting position.

"Smells like Ma's meatloaf, garlic mashed potatoes, and unless my nose deceives me, chocolate cream pie." He carefully opened the box to reveal a made-up plate and set it before her. She immediately went for the pie. He reached over her and lifted the pie out of reach. She gave a growl and reached for the pie. He grinned at her tiny growl.

"Food first, then pie," he said, pushing the box forward.

"Fine," she said, lifting her fork. Her anger faded as she started moaning in appreciation. It was the best food she had ever had. Bite after bite she was in dining heaven. It wasn't until she had plowed through half her meatloaf and polished off all of her potatoes did she look up to find Aleks watching her with a pained look on his face.

"What?" she asked, her fork halfway between her plate and her mouth.

He shifted uncomfortably in his chair, growled, then continued eating.

"Nothing," he said.

She saw the reason for his discomfort and blushed. She didn't mean to get him hot and bothered by moaning over the food. It was just that damn good. She kept peeking over to where the evidence of his arousal was obviously straining the integrity of his uniform zipper. He caught her looking. She gave an impish grin as she blushed, and she saw the tips of his ears turn scarlet.

"Okay, all my food is gone. Pie!" She smiled and handed him her empty plate.

He grinned and passed the pie plate back to her. He still had his sly grin when she picked up her fork and bit into the pie.

"Oh my fucking God!" she yelled. Aleks' mouth dropped and Dr. Claybourne and Connor appeared in the doorway at a run.

"What is it?" Connor asked.

"Are you okay?" Dr. Claybourne asked, moving to her bedside he checked her pulse.

"I'm not mating you, Aleks, I'm mating with your mother. This is the most amazing pie I have ever had!" She wrapped her tongue around her fork and continued to writhe on her bed in food-gasm ecstasy. Connor watched in fascination as Rebecca inhaled her slice of pie. She looked up at the three men with a pout.

"It's gone," she said mournfully. Connor rushed to his cot and got a slice of "extra" pie he brought for himself. He handed it to her with a smile.

"You are awesome!" She took the pie and dug in, this time eating a little slower. Connor grinned as Aleks frowned at his brother. "She should only smile like that for me," he grumbled.

"Since I'm here anyway, let me check your chest," Doc said, trying to maneuver around her fork and plate since she did not stop eating. He placed a hand between her breasts and pressed lightly. She winced a bit and continued to eat her pie. Aleks gave a low growl. Dr. Claybourne rolled his eyes.

"Not taking into account that I am a doctor and would never inappropriately touch a patient, I'm also gay. So this really does nothing for me." He took a pen light and had her look up as he checked her pupils. Aleks seemed to relax a fraction.

"You look good. I'm confident you should be able to go home tomorrow. You'll be sore, but overall you're doing well. Now if you'll excuse me, I also have a slice of Ma's pie waiting for me in my room. If you need me, press the nurse call button. It's connected to the room I have here for when patients stay overnight. Goodnight, everyone." He smiled down at Rebecca and nodded to Aleks and Connor then left.

Rebecca stopped eating her pie and looked down at her plate. Where was home now?

"What is the matter, sweetheart?" Aleks asked, taking the pie plate, he placed it to one side, and sat next to her.

"I don't have a home to go home to. Not really. After the fire I didn't buy another house. I took a furnished apartment. After my boss became my ex-boyfriend, it was determined that my position as head librarian was redundant. That jerk put his "assistant" in charge. That ditz undid all the major changes I had made including the Children's Reading Hour and the tutoring program. She turned the lower level into an internet café. I couldn't watch the years of work I dedicated to the library after my father's death be undone, so I packed up what little I owned and started driving. I haven't had a real home since my father died." She twisted her thumbs around each other.

She felt the mattress dip on the other side as Connor sat down, effectively smushing her between the two brothers. He wrapped an arm around her shoulders and pulled her in to kiss the top of her head.

"I'm not sure if Aleks has had the chance to explain this to you, but you are his mate. That is a bond closer than human marriage. That means you not only have a home now, you have family. So tomorrow when Dr. Claybourne checks you out, you come home to the Arkadion ranch where you will have six brothers waiting to spoil you rotten," he said, smiling down at her.

Rebecca looked between Connor then Aleks and then burst into tears.

"Sweetheart, please calm down, it's okay. Shush." Aleks tried soothing her, but she kept hiccupping and couldn't seem to catch her breath.

"I didn't mean to upset her!" Connor exclaimed sounding frazzled.

Rebecca bawled into her hands. "No, not you, I'm just, I never..." Rebecca couldn't seem to get enough air to get any words out. The crying was starting to hurt her bruised chest. The more upset she got, the more she cried, the more she hurt, which made her upset and the cycle seemed to continue.

Unable to watch his mate so upset, Aleks shooed Connor off the bed so that he could lie down on his side next to her. Connor quietly left, closing the door behind him. Aleks pulled her into the curve of his body and kept running his hand over her hair. After a few more minutes, Rebecca calmed down.

"I'm sorry," she said, snuggling as close to him as she could get.

"For what? Having your world change, being stalked and assaulted? You can cry any time you feel like it and I will be right there so you can soak my shoulder," he said, smiling down at her.

"How does Fate pick mates? I can't think of a single thing I did to deserve being with you," she asked quietly. She knew without a shadow of a doubt that Aleks would be it for her. She already couldn't imagine a life without him. He had quickly become her rock, her solid ground. It seemed almost surreal that she had been rootless with no home or family or love, and now she had all three in spades.

"I'm not sure how Fate picks, but if anyone is undeserving of their mate it's me. I pushed you away and hurt you, and yet here you are in my arms. I'm amazed at your capacity for forgiveness." He rubbed his chin over the top of her head. She wrapped his arm around her waist and scooted backward trying to get comfortable. He inhaled sharply as she grazed his groin.

"Aleks?" she started.

"Yes, love?" he asked.

"What about you, your, umm..." She wiggled a bit and felt his semi erect cock spring to life.

He growled. She grinned then wiggled more, loving the feel of his hard flesh against her lower back.

"Go to sleep, Becca." He placed a hand on her back to keep her from wiggling too much.

"You called me Becca. No one has ever called me that before," she said, smiling.

"Good, I'll be the only one. Now go to sleep," he said.

"But..." she started again.

"Sleep," he said. She huffed.

After a few minutes of silence she said, "We are going to eventually have sex right?"

He sighed. "You're goddamn right we are. Just not when you're bruised and after you've had an emotional meltdown," he replied.

"Okay good, because I really want to see if sex is better than Ashby's quadruple death by chocolate sundae," she said.

Aleks made a painful sound that was somewhere between a moan and growl.

"Night, night, Aleks" she said, yawning.

"You. Are. Evil," he whispered, and she just smiled. She knew that for the rest of their lives she would need to keep him just slightly off-balance to keep the upper hand. She silently congratulated herself. From the occasional whimper she heard she knew she had done well.

CHAPTER NINE

REBECCA WAS MOVING AROUND GIN-GERLY but was reverberating in her seat the next morning as Aleks drove them home. She felt no worse than when she overdid it on the treadmill, but Aleks was taking no chances. He had carried her around all morning after getting checked out of the clinic. They swung by to get her stuff from Liam's. She asked Liam to babysit Sebastian until she was settled at the ranch. She was still wrapping her mind around the word "home," but she liked the idea of it. Home. She kept repeating the word over and over in her mind. She couldn't wait to see where she'd be living.

The drive itself was relaxing. She and Aleks had come a long way in a short amount of time going from rejection to comfortable silence. She looked over to where he sat grinning as he drove, before turning back to look out the window at the dense forest. She decided in the spring when everything was turning green again she would go hiking. Right now the trees were bare and the snow made the forest seem like a winter wonderland.

She still had her face pressed to the window when they drove through an opened gate. The gate itself looked like black wrought iron. The wall that stretched forth on either side of the gate looked to be stones stacked neatly and compactly together. Both stood nearly ten feet high.

As they drove past the gate, Rebecca turned in the passenger seat to look back. The wall extended all the way to the tree line.

"How far does the wall go?" she asked.

Aleks smiled. "It surrounds the entire property."

"That is a pretty big wall," she said.

"It took nearly eight generations of Arkadion men to put up the wall around the property. Each generation after that has chosen some other way to make sure the land is secure. My brothers and I installed motion detectors and a monitoring station in the main house as our contribution. There are six other Arkadia sister sites across the country. After we take over for Ma and Pa, if there is a position open to take care of a town, one of my brothers will go fill it. Otherwise the towns are led by our uncles and cousins. The main house is just ahead," he said, pointing to the huge two story log cabin ahead. It reminded her of the ski lodge she stayed in, her one and only time trying to ski. He maneuvered the car past it.

"My cabin is off to the right. It's nearby without being underfoot. When my parents retire they will move in here and I will take over the main house. My brothers are spread out on the property. I like knowing that they are close by. None of us like the idea of being separated." He looked over and smiled.

"So there are more than the seven of you?" she asked.

Aleks chuckled. "Counting the first cousins there are, in this generation, twenty of us," he replied and her eyes went wide.

"That's a lot of bears," she said.

"You should see us at Christmas." He winked and she gulped.

"My parents were only children. So I have never had a family like that. I mean you have them everywhere, and I couldn't tell you my grandfather's middle name." She sighed then straightened. "Am I the only human?" she asked.

He looked a little uncomfortable. "Yes, but remember it's not by choice. Fate picks our mates," he said, taking her hand and placing a kiss on her knuckles.

"What if they don't like me?" she asked, feeling very small suddenly, which wasn't like her at all.

"You managed to wrap the entire town around your itty-bitty baby finger in less than a day. The rest of my brothers will completely fall in love with you. You already have Ma and Pa under your spell, and they are more than half the battle," he said, laughing, and parked the truck next to a medium-sized two-story home.

"Welcome home," he said, grinning and motioning to the house before them.

Her heart melted. She released her seat belt and leaned over the console and lifted her face to his. Without wasting a second, he closed the gap and took possession of her mouth. His lips were warm, and he expertly demanded her mouth to open.

She sighed softly and wrapped both arms

around his neck. He growled then pulled away for a moment before reaching under him to lift the lever that allowed him to push his seat all the way back. She grinned. He easily lifted her over the console and settled her on his lap. His good intentions placed her sitting sidesaddle. However, she was not having that. She turned and straddled his thighs, placing a knee on either side of his legs on the seat, wedging herself between the console on one side and the door on the other. Looking up she met his eyes, and rotated her hips grinding her body against his. Both of them groaned. Without stopping, she kept her body moving, driving them both crazy. He ran his hands under her sweater and pushed her bra up and out of his way. He deliberately traced around her breast, missing what she wanted him to touch the most. Her pace quickened, and he lifted his hips, causing her to bounce up and down.

"Please," she begged.

He grinned, then wrapped his lips around her pebbled nipple. He dipped one hand into the front of her jeans and found her dripping wet. She groaned and reached between their bodies to wrap her hand around his bulge through his denim. There was no way she was flying without him. He grunted and his breathing became more erratic. She moved her hips mindlessly against his hand as his fingers moved furiously against her tightening nub, and right before she flew apart, she reached lower to cup his sac before drawing her nails up his shaft through the denim. He yelled out and bucked against her.

She collapsed against his chest as he wrapped his

arms around her, both trying to catch their breath. She lifted her head and placed small kisses along his jaw.

"I love you, Becca," he said, burying his face in her neck. She tightened her hold on him.

"I love you too, Aleks. Please don't ever leave me. I don't think I could survive losing someone else," she said.

"I'll never leave you, Becca. You're stuck with your grumpy-ass bear for the rest of our lives." He pulled back to look in her face before giving her another kiss.

"Ready to see your new home?" he asked.

"In a minute, I'm too comfy." She rubbed her face on his chest and snuggled closer.

"Come on, baby girl, we're expected at the main house for dinner, and I don't know about you, but I need to clean up and change my pants." He wiggled his eyebrows at her. She laughed.

"You realize this does not get you off the hook on your promise to cook for me," she said, untangling her body from his. He carefully set her down in the passenger seat.

"I know, I know." He laughed. "How are your bruises?"

"Better today. I'm not as stiff as I was yesterday," she said, smiling.

Aleks grabbed her backpack and suitcase. When he first saw them he had been shocked that she owned so little and promised her a shopping spree.

He unlocked the door then set her bags inside before surprising her by scooping her up and carrying her across the threshold.

She looked around with wide eyes. The design

itself was simple, but everything was clean lines and quality material. She felt like she walked into Pottery Barn. He set her down carefully.

"I love it!" she squealed and began to go from room to room. She gasped when she entered the kitchen. She wheeled around to face him when he came up behind her.

"Do you know what I can cook in a kitchen like this? What time are we expected for dinner?" she said, going through his cabinets and pantry.

"Five o'clock. What are you doing?" he asked.

"I want to see if you have what I need to make my famous Honey Bun cake. I want to take something to dinner," she said, placing the ingredients and pans on the island. "You wash up. By the time you're done, the cake will be baking and then I can jump in," she said, before humming happily. She started dumping ingredients in the bowl and measuring out oil and sugar.

"Watching you hum and putter around the kitchen makes this place finally feel like home."

She looked up and saw his eyes shining. "Because I am your home, not these walls. Now scoot."

She saw him swallow hard then nod. "Right. Shower. Love you Becca."

"Love you too."

She paused in her cake making to watch him walk away. Damn if the man didn't have a fine ass. She sighed lustily, now, where was the sour cream?

CHAPTER TEN

ALEKS GRUMBLED UNDER HIS BREATH as she placed the two cakes in the backseat of his truck. When he got out of the shower he had been bombarded by the amazing aromas coming from their kitchen. He had repeatedly told her that they were keeping the cakes. She had ignored him.

When they got in the truck, he frowned because he could barely reach the steering wheel. Rebecca giggled at his confusion. When he realized why, he leered at her, which caused her to hold her sides and giggle some more.

"We're never getting rid of this truck," he finally said. She smiled. As they got closer to the main house, the more agitated she became. She had nearly worked herself into a panic attack when he reached over and grabbed her hand. She began to calm down.

"Are you sure they'll like me? I'm just a human," she said, looking up at him, worried. He frowned and his chest constricted. He had put that doubt in her eyes and her heart. He would remove it even if it took the rest of their lives together.

"I can't even begin to explain exactly how special you are. Have you ever stopped to think that being the only human in a family of bears is special?" he asked.

"I never thought about it like that," she said, a goofy grin on her face. He smiled back at her, glad to see the shadows were gone from her eyes.

"Come on, let's go meet the horde," he said, and she nodded.

He walked around to her side of the truck and helped her down before reaching in the backseat, grabbing a cake and shutting the door.

"Hem, hem." Rebecca motioned to the door. Sighing he opened the door.

"I brought two cakes, Aleks. Share with your brothers." She pointed to the other cake that he had left in the back seat. He really didn't want to share this amazing-smelling cake with his brothers. But since she was insisting, he grabbed the second cake stacking it on the first.

"They're going to eat it all," he grumbled, and she grinned.

"Good, when the food disappears, that means they like it," she said and took his empty hand. He smiled down at her as they walked hand in hand to the house.

The front door swung open and Pa stood in the doorway. "Look, it's my baby girl coming to visit. What did you bring me?" he asked, his nose going to the air, smelling the delicious aromas coming from the cake.

Rebecca smiled and hugged the older man. His eyes softened and he wrapped an arm around her and steered in into the house.

"Ma, look what I found," he said, taking her coat. Ma walked into the foyer smiling, she wiped her hands on her waist apron.

"Baby girl, how are you feeling? And what is that?" she asked pointing to the pans Aleks held.

"I'm much better today, the truck ride did me a lot of good," she said, giving Aleks a sidelong glance. He immediately proceeded to cough. Pa gave him a few solid whacks on the back.

"Thanks, Pa," he gasped.

"Anytime, son."

Ma winked at Rebecca.

"I brought some cake, I hope that's okay?" Rebecca asked, sounding unsure if the cakes would be welcome.

"Of course that's okay! Food is a rare commodity around here with all the boys over." Ma reassured her.

They walked toward the back of the house to a large open family room that was connected to a kitchen. Immediately they were surrounded by his brothers.

Pa stepped forward and began the introductions.

"In order, we have Benedict, Connor, Duncan, Emmett, Finnian and Gavin." Pa pointed to the first one in line. "Benedict runs a website design company and likes playing around with women too much."

"Pa!" Benedict protested. Rebecca giggled. Pa ignored him and continued.

"Connor you know works in the diner. What you don't know is he is wasting his doctorate in Psychology by working there." Pa shook his head.

"Now, Pa, you know better than anyone how

everyone always comes to the diner to find some-one to talk to. I just happen to be educated enough to help. This way they can't complain if they don't like my advice because I'm only responsible for making their dinner." Connor grinned at Rebecca.

"Humph. The next two are the twins Duncan and Emmet. They own a construction business and the hardware store. They also help me out at the garage when they can." He nodded at the twins. They waved at her.

"Then there is Finnian..." he started.

"Just Finn, call me Finn," Finn interjected.

"Your Ma did not give you a name for you not to use it, boy," Pa said, then continued.

"This is Finnian. He works at the school. He is teaching first grade this year." Pa smiled.

Aleks was willing to bet cash money on the fact that Pa found reasons to stop by the classroom with candy or treats, the smaller the child the harder his Pa fell.

"And last but not least is Gavin. He is our grump-iest bear, but a darn good vet," Pa said with pride shining from his eyes.

Gavin eyed Rebecca up and down then turned to Aleks. "Her hips may be too narrow to birth cubs. She may even be too small for sex." Gavin tilted his head and continued to eye her as if she were a specimen under a microscope. Rebecca's mouth dropped. Pa reached up and cuffed Gavin in the back of the head.

"Gavin!" Aleks growled.

Rebecca recovered and put her hands on her evidently small hips. "I don't know about having cubs, but there better not be any issues with sex."

She looked around the room and realized what she said. Connor snorted first then laughed, which set Rebecca off. Then Finnian joined in while Emmett and Duncan stood there with shit-eating grins wagging their eyebrows at Aleks who grinned right back.

"Okay, boys, leave your sister alone. It's time for dinner," Ma said from the kitchen, and they all filed in to sit down.

Dinner was noisy and fun. Each brother had something funny to share about Aleks, much to her delight and his chagrin. When it came time for dessert, Ma brought out her cakes and cut a piece for everyone. As each boy took a bite, the room quieted.

The table was eerily silent after such a loud and boisterous dinner. Rebecca started to get nervous. She looked over to Aleks, who sat frozen with his fork hanging in midair in front of his face. She felt a flush of panic and quickly took a bite. Everything tasted okay. She looked up at the sound of a chair hitting the floor. Duncan's eyes darkened as he reached for the cake. Emmett intercepted him with a growl. Duncan put him in a headlock and both disappeared into the family room. She heard more noise to her left and saw Connor had Benedict in a similar headlock and they were now on the floor in the kitchen. Finnian and Gavin saw the two cakes on the table and each went to grab one before a low growl froze everyone. Ma let out one more low growl, calmly picked up one of the cakes and put it in front of her. Pa scooted close and accepted the forkfuls that Ma shared with him. The boys resumed their brawls for the remaining cake. Aleks was about to jump in when Rebecca reaches out to stop him. He looked down, worry in his eyes that she might be scared at their barbaric table manners. She wiped away tears of laughter.

"Let's head home," she said. And just like that his eyes lit up. She knew it was because she had called his house, home.

"Okay, baby," he said as they both stepped around his fighting brothers.

"Goodnight Ma, Pa," Rebecca called.

"Goodnight, baby girl," Ma yelled over the boys fighting. Pa waved and smiled.

Once they were in the truck she couldn't hold it in anymore. Holding her sides, she continued to laugh out loud. She felt tears rolling down her face. He went to buckle her in, and she slid down the seat and onto the floor trying to catch her breath. He gave up and drove slowly back to their house. She was still cackling when he pulled up into their driveway. He put the truck in park as she started to calm down.

"We're not always like that. It's just that bear shifters are known for loving their sweets," he said, sounding embarrassed.

"It was fun. That's how family should be," she said, climbing into her seat.

"They were kind of rough," he admitted.

"They are guys," she said simply.

"It was kind of funny."

She shook her head. "Their tumbling wasn't why I was laughing," she admitted.

"Why were you laughing?" Aleks asked.

"Because I made three cakes," she said, grinning up at her mate.

Aleks froze, then darted out of the truck and into the house leaving her sitting in the driveway. Rebecca smiled and made her way inside. She found him in their den, in his recliner with the entire cake in his lap.

"I can't believe you're my mate and you can make this cake," he said, eating forkful after forkful. She watched in utter amazement as the cake began to quickly disappear.

"I may have to ration out the cake for favors," she remarked.

He grinned up at her, finishing the last slice. She was slightly concerned with how fast he inhaled the entire cake. He stood slowly, setting the pan aside.

"What kind of favors would you require?" he asked, his deep voice making her shiver.

He stalked closer to her, his eyes dark. When he nonchalantly removed his shirt she nearly swallowed her tongue. Her imagination in no way prepared her for him. His shoulders were broad and his chest and abs were perfectly defined. His skin looked golden, and he had a dusting of dark hairs over his chest in a trail down his stomach. Subconsciously she licked her lips. When his hands reached for his pants, she stepped back and pulled her shirt over her head. He froze. She stood there, her shoulders bare except for the thin satin straps of her bra. Her full breasts were encased in pink lace. She took advantage of his immobility and one-upped him by quickly removing her jeans. She stood before him in her pink lace bra and boy shorts, her sex-kitten act fading in the face of the reality that she was nearly naked before him. She felt her body flush with embarrassment.

He stepped forward and ran a finger down her neck and shoulder. She shivered again. He picked her up and carried her upstairs to his room. Gently he set her on her feet next to the bed. He moved his hands over her shoulders and pushed the straps down her arms. He reached behind her and released the clasp. The bra fell to the floor. He seemed to drink in the sight of her breasts. He took both in his hands and kneaded them gently as her head fell back. He leaned forward and took one nipple into his hot mouth. He rolled his tongue over it and pulled on it with harder suction. He released it and then blew a breath of cool air over it.

He dropped to his knees and pulled her lace boy shorts down over her hips. She carefully stepped out of them. He lightly touched her soft curls. Her hands came down to his shoulders in an effort to stay upright. He leaned forward and pressed a soft kiss on her mound. He stood, scooped her up and tossed her into the middle of his oversized king bed before removing his jeans. She laughed as she bounced, but it was cut short at the sight of him crawling toward her. Her eyes widened as she saw his cock for the first time. She swallowed hard and licked her lips.

She lay there and watched him advance, her knees pressed tightly together.

He smiled and shook his head.

"You are keeping your honey from me, baby girl, and you know how bears are about their honey." He placed a hand on each knee and parted her thighs. When he looked down, his eyes hooded. She squirmed under his gaze. He raised an eyebrow and began to push her boundaries. He placed his hands on her inner thighs and spread them wide until she lay completely exposed. She gasped and tried to close her legs.

"Aleks!" she protested, and he chuckled.

"Easy, baby girl. I need to get acquainted with what is now mine," he said and lowered his head and kissed her rounded belly. He slowly kissed his way down her mound. Using his thumbs, he spread her folds wide, exposing her completely. He flattened his tongue and ran it from the bottom of her slit to her clit then stopped as his canines dropped.

"Mine!" he growled.

"Yours," she breathed.

He returned to run his tongue up and down, drinking her down. He nibbled on her small nub, and she went wild above him. Her hands found his hair and she held on. He wrapped his lips around her clit and pulled as he eased a finger in her tight channel. She screamed and clamped down on his finger. She shook then came hard.

"That's one," he said before nipping the inside of her thighs.

One? She tried to catch her breath. She felt his teeth on her inner thigh and sighed. She was just starting to breathe normally when he inserted another finger. Unable to help herself, she moved her hips. She wanted something else, something more.

"More," she whispered.

He shook his head.

"Not yet, I'm not going to hurt you." He plunged two fingers in and out of her channel slowly. She felt something else starting build.

"Pull on your nipples, baby. Let me see how much you want me," he said.

She brought her hands up to cup both breasts and pulled on her nipples. She felt electricity travel down her body straight to her clit. She continued to pull and moved her hips, wanting to take his fingers deeper.

She slowed when she felt herself being stretched and looked down. He had added a third finger. Very slowly he continued the in-and-out motion. Soon the burn began to fade and her pleasure came back. He brought her to the brink then backed away. He teased her mercilessly.

"Please!" she cried out, tears in her eyes.

It seemed he was waiting on her desperation. She looked in his eyes as he quickly replaced his fingers with the head of his cock and began to slowly sink into her. If she thought she had been stretched before, she was wrong. He was stretching her too much!

"Too much!" she cried out.

He stopped and pulled back slowly. He waited until she relaxed and then began to push forward again. He repeated this over and over. She noticed that each time it was getting easier and he was going deeper. She wanted him. She wanted all of him.

"More," she said, looking into his face. He nodded and she noticed his eyes had shifted to a dark brown, almost black. He pushed forward, going the deepest he had ever been. It hurt, but she knew that it would get worse before it got better. She ground her teeth and looked back up.

"More," she whispered. He must have seen the determination in her face. He withdrew and plunged all the way in, pushing past the tight flesh that had been keeping them apart. She tensed up and grabbed his arms that were on either side of her body, holding him up.

"Relax, baby," he said, his voice deeper than usual and rougher.

She relaxed and tried pushing out. He slid in a fraction deeper. They both moaned. After a minute she looked up at him.

"Okay," she said. He pulled out then plunged in again. There was a bit of pain, but it faded quickly. He slid in again and again, his pace quickening. The pain was gone now and the fire that he had started came roaring back. She began to move her hips up to meet him as he thrust forward again and again. There was so much coiled strength and tension in the man above her. Knowing that she was the cause of it spurred her on, she opened her legs wider to accept every inch of him.

He lowered himself so that he rested on his forearms, his hips still snapping forward. His nose nuzzled her neck, and she felt his teeth graze her shoulder.

"More," she said and brought her legs up to wrap around his waist. She gasped as this changed the angle.

"More, please, God, more, I'm almost there, Aleks please!" She couldn't get him deep enough on her own.

Finally taking her at her word, he began to slam into her repeatedly. She held on as he pushed into her body time and time again. This is what she had been waiting for all her life!

"Yes! Don't stop, don't ever stop!" She cried out, clawing at his shoulders. His pace began to quicken, and she knew he was close. Without thought, she clamped down and he hit that elusive spot deep inside her. As her orgasm exploded, she felt him lean forward and bury his teeth in her shoulder. With each pull from his mouth, she felt as if he were pulling her soul into his. In the space of a single heartbeat, both souls expanded as one orgasm ended and another began. A new soul was created then split as a portion of each one settled back into their hearts. Time resumed as they slammed back into reality, and the pain of his canines sent her into a tailspin of another orgasm. She screamed out her final release, and then her world went dark.

When she woke, he was seated at the end of the bed, his elbows on his knees and his face in his hands.

"What's wrong?" she asked, sitting up. She winced but then smiled. She had earned her discomfort.

Go me! I'm such a slut now. She giggled at her own thoughts.

He turned around and her good mood evaporated. He looked as if someone died.

"Oh my God, what happened?" she asked, scooting next to him.

"I hurt you," he said brokenly.

"Not really, you made me feel real good, baby," she said, smiling and kissing his shoulder.

He turned and looked at her. She could see his eyes were wide and he looked kinda shocky.

"Talk to me, baby, please." She hugged his arm, bringing it between her breasts.

He pointed to her shoulder and at her legs. When she looked down, she saw a small smear of blood. She knew exactly where his mind was, and she didn't like it. She stood and climbed up so she straddled him and could look him in the face.

"Aleks, listen to me. I am not her. I am okay. I may be human, but evidently I can take a pounding." She smiled then winked at him. She saw some of the fear leave his eyes and his mouth twitched.

"That's not funny," he said, wrapping his arms around her waist.

"Yes, it is. I'm a little sore, but it's a good sore, like how your muscles feel after a really good deep-tissue massage." She grinned. "You definitely massaged some deep tissue." She giggled. Finally he smiled then laughed.

"You're really okay?" he asked, holding her close.

"I'm more than okay, I am perfect. I have everything I have ever wanted. You are everything I waited for and more." She cuddled him, and when she put her ear to his chest, she heard his heart beat begin to slow down and regulate.

He fell backwards, taking her with him. They laughed and got under the covers.

"So when can we do that again?" she asked, and he groaned.

"Let's give your body a chance to recover," he said, pulling her into his arms.

"So, in the morning?" she asked.

"Go to sleep," he said.

"Tomorrow afternoon? A nooner?..." she started.

"Sleep," he said.

"But..."

"Sleep," he repeated kissing the back of her neck.

"Okay." She sighed. "I love you, my grumpy-ass bear," she said.

"I love you too, my itty-bitty human." She smiled and fell asleep.

CHAPTER ELEVEN

"WE DIDN'T HAVE ANY PROBLEMS having sex!" Rebecca stuck out her tongue at Gavin the next morning when the entire family was eating breakfast at the main house. He looked up startled and dropped his fork. Aleks began to choke on his waffle, turning a deep red, and Connor and the twins began to laugh, leaning on each other in their seats in an effort to stay upright. Pa smiled down into his plate, and Ma was beaming.

"Good for you, baby girl! Did you want another waffle?" she asked.

"Yes please," Rebecca said.

"Rebecca!" Aleks said when he could breathe.

"What? It's not like they don't know we're having sex. I've moved in. It's not like I'm in the guest room," she said, biting into her bacon.

"But still it's my Ma and Pa!" he said.

"They have seven boys, Aleks, I'm pretty sure they know all about sex," she said, munching away at her breakfast. All seven boys at the table shuddered and made faces. It was their Ma and Pa after all.

"I don't want to know," Aleks said, holding up a hand. Rebecca just giggled and ate her waffles.

"What are you going to do today, baby girl?" Ma asked.

"I'm going back to the library. Some of the older volumes are drool worthy, but the entire place needs to be brought into the twenty-first century. I don't think any new books have been brought in, in over thirty years," she said. Aleks was staring at her.

"What?" she asked.

"Baby, you're my mate," Aleks said.

"Yes, I know," she said, looking at him.

"You don't have to work. Being Alpha Mother will take a lot of your time," he said. She would have thought he was joking except for the extremely serious look on his face.

"So what you're basically saying is that what I want doesn't matter and my job is to be your mate?" she asked carefully.

He was nodding absently until Pa cleared his throat, quickly shaking his head at Aleks.

"No! I mean no, baby, but maybe you would like to take a break and enjoy learning about the town," he said, and his Pa started nodding his head.

"What better way to learn about the town than to dive into the town's old newspapers and archives?" she asked, taking another bite of her waffles.

"What about working at the diner with Ma and Connor," he said. She read between the lines. 'Where you will be safe.'

"No offense, Ma, but I do not want to work at the diner." She finished her breakfast and looked up at him. "Aleks, I am not sitting around the house naked all day making you cake. As short lived as that fantasy was, wave it bye-bye," she said.

"Hmmm, God, that cake was good," Aleks said, smiling.

"How would you know? You left after only one bite." Connor laughed. Evidently he had gotten the largest portion of the second cake and had been bragging all morning.

"Because she made three cakes. I had one all to myself." Aleks grinned at his brothers.

"Son of a bitch! It's not fair. She is perfect and can make that amazing cake!" Duncan exclaimed.

"Duncan! Language!" Ma said.

"Sorry, Ma," he said, still pouting.

Rebecca grinned and thought of a way to get what she wanted. She turned to Aleks.

"Now, I know you have to work, but you'll be worried about what I'll be doing." He went to speak but she held up a hand.

"If one of your brothers promises to spend the day with me so you won't worry, I'll pick up ingredients to make another cake for that good brother," she said, smiling at the men staring at her.

Instantly the boys started to argue.

"You have to work!" Duncan said.

"You do too, asshole!" Connor replied.

"Boys!"

On and on it went. Finally at Ma's insistence the boys made their way outside to brawl it out. Rebecca looked worried that they were fighting, but Aleks looked amused.

"You were worried they wouldn't like you," he said.

"They just really like the cake," she said, wincing

as Emmett's head connected to the ground.

"And here I thought I had a smart mate, a genius even," he said, cupping her cheek.

"They are fighting for the chance to watch over you."

She turned and quickly ran outside, tackling Connor. "I've never had brothers before and y'all are the best ever! I promise to be a good sister and make you as much cake as you want!" She started trying to hug them all at the same time, practically tackling the group, shocking the brothers.

Aleks was beginning to see a pattern here. Rebecca never felt something just a little bit. What she felt she felt with her entire being. When she loved, she loved completely. He looked on as his younger brothers scrambled to surround Rebecca and pat her on the head trying to get her to calm down. It was funny to watch, since he knew that she was overwhelmed at the love she felt for them.

"You going to save them?" Pa asked from the doorway where they stood.

"Nah, it's good for them," he said magnanimously, hooking his thumbs into his belt loops, rocking back on his heels. Pa chuckled.

"It's not good for her to get worked up like that, especially if she's pregnant," Ma said calmly from behind them.

Aleks's face drained of any color and he lurched forward to scoop Rebecca up and cuddle her. All six brothers stayed around her smiling and joking on Aleks. Aleks looked back and saw Pa grinning.

"You are evil woman. But you do sure know what these boys need. They are lucky to have a Ma like you," Pa said as he wrapped his arm around her waist.

"They are good boys," she said simply.

"That they are," he said and watched his boys and his baby girl.

"Thanks for taking me, Gavin," Rebecca said as they climbed out of his SUV. Rebecca smiled at Rian and Damian as they got out of the back seat. Rebecca wanted to go to the used book store in the neighboring town to search for gently used books for the library. She could get new, but she figured she could afford a lot more getting used. When Aleks realized he couldn't escort her shopping because of a public works meeting, he enlisted Gavin, Rian, and Damian to act as escorts.

"I needed to see if the anatomy charts I ordered were in anyway," he said shrugging. Rian rolled his eyes. Gavin was blunt, but sweet in his own way.

"Damian and I are going to see if they have the new man-love books we ordered. Don't leave the store. If a hyena comes in we'll be able to smell them a mile away," Rian said as Rebecca started to go through the shelves.

Damian nodded. "Lord knows they smell enough." Damian shuddered.

"Come on, Damian, the man-love books are calling for me," Rian said, heading towards the counter. Damian laughed and caught up with him.

Rebecca had just started on the second shelf when she felt someone standing close behind her. She turned around and stepped back into the shelf of books. A man was grinning down at her.

"You know when you bend over like that I can see your pretty blue lace underwear," he said. His eyes were bloodshot and filled with lust. Rebecca felt her stomach roll at the idea of this man seeing anything so intimate of hers.

"Enjoy the peep show, because that's all you will ever see," she said, looking over his shoulder desperately hoping to see Rian or Damian.

"Come on, baby, I can take real good care of you," he said, rubbing his crotch. Rebecca shuddered.

"I'm sorry, I have a ma... a husband," she said.

The man looked at her empty left hand and his eyes narrowed.

"You're a lying bitch. You're not even wearing a ring. What, you think you're too good for me?" He grabbed her arm and yanked her close.

"Get your hands off me!" she exclaimed, trying to pull away.

"I think you like my hands on you and you like it rough," he said, leaning his face close to hers. Just when she was about to scream, the man's face went pale and his hand released her. He looked past her and started to shake. She felt someone beside her gently pull her backwards. She turned to her left and gasped. The man who held her gently was exquisite. His black hair held a slight curl and lightly brushed his shoulders. He was tall, but his frame was lean and firm, not bulky. His eyes glowed red. The man stumbled backward and ran out of the store. If she weren't so concerned about the man beside her, she would have laughed at the comical way he tripped out of the door.

"Are you well?" The man turned his gaze to her and his eyes went from red to a pale teal to a brilliant blue. His voice soothed her, calming her nerves.

"Yes, thank you so much! That guy was just creepy," she said. He smiled and nodded in agreement. She eyed him carefully. She knew he wasn't a shifter since Gavin and the others didn't smell him.

"What exactly are you?" she asked, looking up at him. He smiled and two white but sharp-looking fangs peeked out from his sensual lips.

"Oh my goodness, you're a vampire, aren't you. That is amazing, I've always wanted to meet one," she said, grinning up at him.

"You want to let me feed, don't you, to thank me," he said, taking both her hands in his, his eyes never leaving hers.

The feeling of calmness spread. She looked down at their hands and saw he wore a heavy and ornate ring.

"That is so cool! That ring has to be an antique. Where did you get it?" she asked, tilting her head at him. A surprised look crossed his face.

"You're mated, aren't you?" he asked, stepping back as he dropped her hands.

"Yes, he's a bear. Why?" she asked.

"My gaze didn't work on you. It doesn't work on strong paranormals or their mates," he explained.

"Oh. Did you still need...you know." She tilted her neck. His eyes widened and he took another step backwards.

"No, that's okay, I'll be fine. Here is a flyer for my club. We're new in town. It's paranormal only. You and your mate are welcome to come." He handed her a printed post-card-sized flyer.

"Let them know Gabriel invited you, and they will take good care of you," he said.

"Thank you, Gabriel, I'm Rebecca," she said, taking the flyer and tucking it in her bag.

He took her hand and raised it to her lips.

"It was a distinct pleasure to meet you, Rebecca," he said. The sound of a stack of books tumbling had Rebecca turning away for a second. When she turned back, he was gone. Shaking her head, she made her way to the counter. Gavin had three laminated posters rolled up under his arm as Rian and Damian excitedly discussed their new purchases.

"I absolutely love your world. Shifters and vampires are freaking awesome!" Rebecca said when she got to their group.

"Glad you feel that way, because you're stuck with us," Rian said, laughing.

She struck up a conversation with the store owner about placing a bulk order. She arranged for it to be packaged and delivered to the store and for her to be called when it was ready to be picked up. She couldn't wait to get home to tell Aleks about her day.

"Rebecca, Gavin, boys, dinner's ready, go wash up," Ma said, pointing to the bathroom. Gavin, Rian, and Damian headed to the bathroom to wash their hands, and Rebecca, not wanting to wait, went to the kitchen sink. Hands washed, she looked around the family room, trying to find Aleks. She was spun around and a warm pair of lips crushed hers. Sighing, she wrapped her arms around Aleks and held on while he kissed the life out of her.

"I missed you, baby," he whispered before teasing her neck. She melted in his arms.

"I missed you too!" she said as he led her to the table to sit down. Everyone was spooning out food onto their plates.

"Liam dropped Sebastian off at the house today while you were out. That cat doesn't like me," he said, sitting down.

"Liam likes you," she said, sitting next to him. He laughed.

"Not that cat, the other one, Sebastian. That thing growled at me," Aleks explained. Rebecca looked at him, shocked.

"Sebastian is the sweetest cat I've ever seen." Her eyes narrowed. "What did you do to him?" she asked.

"Nothing, I swear," Aleks said, his eyes wide. His brothers and Rian were laughing at the end of the table. He growled at them.

"Maybe he is scared by your growling. You are very growly," Rebecca said, scooping out some potatoes.

"Is growly a word?" Aleks asked no one in particular. "So besides an extremely boring public works meeting and getting hissed at by Liam's Mini-Me, my day was peachy. How about you, baby?" he asked.

"My day was crazy," she said, digging into her corn.

"Craziness at a bookstore. I can't wait to hear," Aleks said, his eyes dancing with laughter.

"Well I was looking at the quality of books that the store had to offer when this creepazoid came up behind me saying he could see my underwear. Then he was grabbing his crotch and saying he could show me a good time. I told him I had a husband, but he got mad and said I was lying because I wasn't wearing a ring. Then he grabbed my arm, and I think he was about to kiss me when this absolutely gorgeous man showed up. His eyes were all glowy red, and I swear he made creepazoid piss his pants. Come to find out he was a vampire. He tried to get me to feed him until he realized I was a mate and couldn't do his mind-control thing on me. I offered to feed him anyway since he saved me and all, but he said that was okay. He said his name was Gabriel and gave me a flyer to his club. He said it was for paranormals only. I want to go. Do you think we can go tomorrow?" she asked hopefully.

Everyone stared at her.

"Aleks, calm down, she didn't know," Pa said in the most serious voice Rebecca had ever heard from him. She looked around and everyone's face was frowning. Rian, Damian, and Gavin looked especially pale.

"What? What's wrong?" she asked.

"What's wrong is you offered to feed that damn bloodsucker," Aleks yelled. Rebecca flinched. Aleks had never yelled at her before.

"So? He saved me, Aleks, I was trying to be nice," she said. Aleks's eyes had shifted, and she noticed his hands had shifted into claws. He stood, knocking his chair to the floor, his clawed hands flat on the table's surface.

"Only you would find a way to be saved in a damn bookstore," he said, growling.

"What in the hell is that supposed to mean? It's not like I go looking for trouble you know," Rebecca said indignantly, her eyes filling with tears.

"She shouldn't have needed a bloodsucker to come to her rescue. Where in the hell were the three of you!" he demanded, his gaze swinging to where Rian, Damian, and Gavin sat.

"Don't get mad at them! If I had a wedding ring he probably wouldn't have even approached me," she said, her arms crossed over her chest.

He turned to face her.

"Human marriage is nothing compared to the bond created when mates are claimed. Humans can fall in and out of love and divorce. The bond of human marriage is a façade. It's a stupid human custom!" His canines dropped and it looked like his body was expanding.

"Son, go! Out back now!" Pa yelled, pushing him out the back door. Aleks ran for the back door as a human anguished yell turned into a loud roar. Connor and Duncan started pulling off their clothes and shifted before running out the back.

Rebecca looked around the room. Everyone showed a mixture of concern and sadness. She was about to speak when the doorbell rang. Benedict went to answer the door. Rebecca couldn't get Aleks' tortured yell out of her mind. She didn't even realize she was shaking until a warm pair of arms wrapped around her. She looked up, tears streaming down her face to see Ashby sitting there with a kind smile. Unable to hold back, she threw her arms around his neck and began to sob. Nicholas stood behind them running a hand over her hair.

"Come on, sweetie, you can stay with me. Aleks won't be coming back tonight. He'll probably sleep in bear form with his brothers outside," Ashby said, wiping away her tears.

"She belongs here, Ashby," Ma said.

"Ma, I don't doubt for one second that you love Rebecca and think of her as a daughter. But I also don't doubt that between the two, Aleks will always come first. She is still new to this family and feels outnumbered. I'll take her to my home and calm her down," he said, standing and pulling Rebecca to his side. Rian and Damian stood behind them with Nicholas.

"You're acting unusually brave, fox," Ma said, looking at him closely. "How did you know to come here tonight?" she asked.

"I was on my way here to speak with Rebecca about volunteering at the library. I don't have her cell phone number, and Aleks's house phone kept going to voicemail. I felt panic and fear from my Alpha Mother, so Nic and I headed here. She gives me strength and courage to be who I am," Ashby said, stepping forward with Rebecca, facing down Ma, who now had Benedict and Emmett standing behind her.

"You have never received any strength from me," she said carefully.

"I never said I did," Ashby walked Rebecca toward the door.

"We'll stay with them tonight," Damian said, motioning to Rian, and all five left the house.

CHAPTER TWELVE

"HE HATES ME!" REBECCA CRIED from between Ashby and Nic. Rian had offered to drive, and Damian rode shotgun.

"He doesn't hate you. His bear is riding him hard. The first couple years after mating, our animals are extremely protective and possessive. When he heard that you were threatened and then in the company of vampires, I think his bear broke free," Ashby said, rubbing her arms.

"Why did you offer to feed a bloodsucker, Rebecca? I thought you were happy with Aleks," Damian asked.

"He was hungry and he saved me. It seemed like the polite thing to do," she said, sniffling.

Damian, Rian, Nic, and Ashby groaned.

Ashby turned to her. "Rebecca, offering to feed a vampire is equivalent to offering them sex. Even a quick feeding like you offered would at least be considered a blow job. Vampires are highly sexual. Most of them are bisexual so that they can have multiple types of partners and no restrictions on their feeding sources."

"Oh my God, I thought it was like offering him a sandwich!" The men groaned again.

"You're new to our world. There are things you don't know. Why didn't you tell me or Rian about the vampire? We could have at least coached you on what and how to tell Aleks," Damian asked.

"Y'all are shifters. He was a vampire. I guess I didn't think it was a big deal and I did say that I thought your world was awesome and did mention vampires," she said, shrugging.

"We really need to work on re-establishing your new sense of normal. Shifters and hyena attacks... normal. Bloodsucking vampires wanting to chomp on your neck, not normal! Not normal!" Rian ranted. Damian smacked him upside the head.

"Ow!" Rian said, putting the car in park. Rebecca smiled.

The car sat in front of Ashby's ice cream parlor in town. She looked up.

"You live here?" she asked.

He nodded. "There's an apartment upstairs. Come on, little mother, let's get you settled," he said taking her hand.

"Ashby, Damian and I will take the guest room, if that's okay?" Rian asked as they entered the small but impeccably well kept apartment.

"That's fine. Rebecca, Nic, and I will be in the master," he answered.

Rian and Damian looked at each other.

"Do you think it's a good idea for y'all to share a bed? I mean Aleks' bear is freaking out enough as it is," Rian said.

Ashby snorted. "If he feels threatened by me, then he has bigger problems than his bear," Ashby replied smiling ruefully.

"Why wouldn't he feel threatened by you? You're absolutely gorgeous," Rebecca said, yawning.

Rian and Damian shook their heads. Nicholas smiled sadly.

"Because he is a bear and an Arkadion, and I'm just a fox with no long familial lines," Ashby explained.

"People are more than their animals and family names. You are an amazing person, Ashby. Don't let anyone make you feel any different," Rebecca said.

Ashby's eyes teared up. "I'm glad you're my Alpha Mother." He rubbed his cheek against hers as she giggled.

"You mentioned that back at the ranch. What do you mean, Ashby?" Damian asked, making himself at home on the loveseat with Rian.

"When we met, I offered Rebecca my allegiance and she accepted. Just because Ma is the town's Alpha Mother doesn't mean she has the fealty of all the townspeople. I never felt like Ma would look after me, so I never swore my allegiance to her. But I knew from the moment I met Rebecca she would defend and protect me. Leona is the town's historian. She will have a record of previous Alpha Mothers and who pledged themselves to them," Ashby said, cuddling up to Rebecca on the couch.

"Leona? Really?" Rebecca asked.

"Leona may not act it, but she is more reliable than she looks. She has seen many Alpha Mothers run this town. She may have seen previous examples of this happening," Ashby said.

"I'd like to pledge my allegiance to you, Alpha Mother," a quiet voice said from Rebecca's other side. She turned to face Nicholas. He was an embarrassed shade of pink and looking down at his lap.

"I..I.. don't know what it means to be an Alpha Mother. What if I screw you guys up?" she said feeling terrified. This was different than the fun of discovering new things that shifters could do. They were depending on her for protection and leadership. It scared her to death that she would fail them.

"You are already doing a great job, Rebecca. You see us as people. Not as lions or wolves or foxes. Just as people. You care about us and want us safe and happy. There's not much more we can expect from you than that. A lot of Alpha Mothers concentrate on the town, it being financially secure, or the politics of fitting in with the other prides, packs, and the council. They harbor a preference for bears even if it's subconscious. But you're human. You don't have any preconceived ideas about what is good or bad. It's why for the first time in my life I tied myself to a leader. You are the first and only one I trust," Ashby said, taking her hand.

"It's also why I want to pledge myself to you. I trust you, Rebecca, to take care of us. *All* of us," Nicholas said, taking her other hand. Rebecca turned to Damian and Rian.

"We trust you too, kiddo, but before we can pledge anything we have to discuss it with our Alpha," Rian said, smiling.

"I don't have that restriction, unless you don't want me," Nicholas asked hesitantly.

"I do! Hmm. How do I do this? Liam was there last time," she said.

Nicholas tilted his head, exposing his neck.

"Just do what you did with me and lay your lips on his neck. There has to be an intent to bond. With me, I dedicated myself to you as my Alpha and you offered your protection, because you said I was your friend and would do it anyway. It will be the same with Nicholas," Ashby said.

"Okay, here goes nothing," Rebecca said, leaning forward, and gently placed her lips on his neck. She knew that she would protect Ashby and Nicholas and care for them because they were precious to her as her friends. Nicholas gasped and then sighed happily. Rebecca felt another shift in her heart and the connection to Ashby and Nicholas. Nicholas had tears streaming down his face.

"I feel like I've come home," he said brokenly as Rebecca and Ashby hugged him.

"I think we all have," Ashby said.

"I wonder what Aleks will think about you two being pledged to Rebecca," Rian mused out loud.

"Well, after I explain that I didn't know about the whole vampire thing and then let him grovel over the whole 'you could find a way to get in trouble at a book store' and 'stupid human custom' comments, I'll see what he thinks." Rebecca sighed. "Being mated is hard." She yawned again, snuggling down between Nic and Ashby. It felt right being with them, like being with lost family.

"You've had to deal with discovering about shifters, vampires, and other paranormals. Then we have hyenas going even more bat-shit crazy than they normally are. Usually finding and claiming your mate is an orgasm-a-thon," Rian said. Rebecca giggled.

"Oh oh, does that mean Aleks has been taking

care of business?" Rian asked, wagging his eye-brows.

"He always does. I miss him. I wish I could have been there for him. If I had been a shifter I could have shifted and stayed with him," she said softly.

The men exchanged sad looks, because she was right. As a shifter she could have stayed with him. As a human she would have been in danger. Rian cleared his throat.

"So do you think you will get your wedding?" he asked. She looked up surprised.

"I don't know. I hope so. God, what if he says yes? I'm so stupid. Can you imagine the wedding? There would be no one to walk me down the aisle or sit on my side of the church. I should have kept my dumb mouth shut." She sighed and closed her eyes. She had pissed off Aleks to the point that he had to shift and she could no longer be around him, practically offered a vampire a blow job, and brought up a wedding that really wasn't needed.

Determined to lighten the mood, Rian contin-ued.

"Who cares about that? Pa would shit car-sized bricks if you asked him to walk you down the aisle and probably bawl like a baby the whole way down. You have me and Damian on your side, plus most of the pride would definitely sit on your side of the church to avoid those grumpy bears. The most important thing is the dress!" he said, clap-ping his hands.

"Oh my God, you guys have to help me with this if he asks! I've never even been in a wedding," Rebecca exclaimed.

"You mean it? You trust us?" Rian squealed as

Damian broke into a wide grin.

"This town is so boring. You come in and everything is changing. I get to plan a wedding! Oh my God, we have to go to New York for the dress, nothing off the rack. I need to call Kate," he said, whipping out his cell phone.

"Rian, it's close to midnight," Rebecca said.

"Girl, please, they are probably between rounds two and three." He waited as the phone rang. "Katie! Yes I know what time it is. Yes I knew what you'd probably be doing. Fine, I won't tell you about the wedding I get to plan." He held the phone away from his ear as a loud screech of "whaaat" came over the phone line.

"Tell him it will still be there in the morning." Rian giggled evilly then placed the phone on speaker.

"Rebecca, is it true are you getting married?" Kate asked, somewhat breathless.

"Well not yet. It came up in an argument tonight. Aleks is actually kinda mad at me at the moment, but I'm hoping he'll marry me," Rebecca said.

"Oh my goodness, I want to help. Please let me help!" Kate pleaded. There was a muffled sound of someone getting hit.

"Bran, hush, we were resting between sessions anyway," Kate said and Rebecca blushed.

"I was hoping you would be my maid of honor. You've become like a sister to me," Rebecca said quietly.

Silence filled the room. Everyone stared at the phone. Finally an extremely loud sniff heralded squeals and sobs from Kate's line. The men let out their collective breath.

"This is so amazing!" Rian said, bouncing around.

"Of course I'll be your maid of honor. Who will be your bridesmaids?" she asked.

Rebecca hesitantly looked at Nic and Ashby then looked away.

"We'd be honored as long as we don't have to wear a dress," Nic said, laughing. Ashby smiled.

"Thank you! And Rian and Damian are the wedding coordinators. I feel like we're missing something," Rebecca said then looked down at her empty hand.

"Crap! I'm missing the damn groom. Boys, let's head back to the ranch. Y'all can stay until Aleks comes back, and then I have some major begging to do and it's going to involve cakes. Come on!" She jumped up.

"Go get him, Rebecca, and call me first thing in the morning. I am dying to hear what happens!" Kate said.

The guys got up grinning, and headed towards the door.

CHAPTER THIRTEEN

ALEKS WOKE UP THE NEXT morning with his brothers in the small cabin they had on the property for when they spent the night out shifted. All three had passed out there when they had exhausted their bears.

"God, I forgot how bad you snore. I feel sorry for Rebecca," Connor said, opening his eyes.

"I hope you're not still mad at her. She didn't know about the vampire thing," Emmett said, eyes still closed.

"I was never mad at her," Aleks said confused, getting dressed.

Connor snorted. "You could have fooled us. Your eyes and hands shifted and you were yelling at her. I'd be surprised if her stuff is still at your house," Connor said, pulling on his sweats.

"Oh God, you're right. She would think I was mad at her. Why did I say that about human weddings?" He groaned into his hands.

"You were probably still pissed at the human assaulting her and the vampire coming on to her," Emmett said, grabbing his sweats and stepping back, hands up in the universal "my bad" gesture as Aleks growled.

"See, you're still snarly," Emmett said, heading to the small kitchenette to make coffee.

"She mates me and she's attacked what...like three times? Thank God the vampire she volunteered to feed was honorable enough not to take her up on her offer, but ultimately that would have been my fault for not explaining things to her." Aleks stared down at the floor.

"She's a part of our world now, Aleks. There's no taking that back. But you're not alone, you have us, and Ma and Pa, and from the looks of things, Liam, his pride, and Kate and her pack watching over her. As far as the wedding bit is concerned, you know human females dream of getting married the way our people dream of finding their mates. She fulfilled your dream, go fulfill hers. Get a ring and ask her to marry you. Done," Emmett said, grinning proudly at the solution he found.

"It's not that easy," Aleks said.

"Why not?" Emmett asked. "You love her, she loves you. You mated her, she's mated to you. She wants to get married, so marry her. It's one more tie that will hold you together. She keeps tripping over shifter and paranormal rules. Sit down and explain them to her. Then fuck like bunnies. See? Easy," Emmett said.

"You know as crazy as that sounds, I think he's right, somewhere in there," Connor said, smiling.

"I especially like the fuck like bunnies part," Aleks said, grinning. "So, get a ring, beg forgiveness, and then explain rules before resuming post-mating sex?" Aleks asked.

"Sounds like a plan to me." Connor grinned.

"Being mated is harder than I thought it would be," Aleks said.

"Anything worth having requires some work, Aleks," Emmett said.

"When did you get so damn smart?" Aleks asked, smiling.

"I've been reading," Emmett said.

"Does Ma know you can read?" Connor asked then ducked as Emmett swiped at him.

"Asshole," Emmett said, laughing.

"Okay, so plan is set. I think I know where to get a ring too," he said.

"Go get her!" Connor said, pushing him out the door.

"Think they'll be ok?" Emmett asked.

"He's following your plan," Connor said.

"I heard that!" Aleks yelled back at them.

Aleks patted his shirt pocket where his grand-mother's ring sat. He grinned remembering the happy looks on his parents' faces when he asked for the ring. He pulled up in his driveway and frowned. Ashby's car was still here. He also smelled Rian, Damian, and Nicholas.

He walked up to the front door and heard Rebecca say, "No, that one goes in the family room, and that one goes in the bedroom. It has a special meaning." Letting his curious nature take over, he walked around to the window and peeked in to see his mate wearing a short robe positioning a cake in the den. He frowned not liking other males around his mate when she wasn't dressed, he quickly made his way back to the front door and unlocked the deadbolt. When he opened the door, Damian, Rian, Ashby, and Nicholas practically ran him over leaving.

"Good luck!" Rian said, winking, and then the group of them jumped into Ashby's car and took off like a bat out of hell. What in the world was his mate up to?

"Rebecca?" he asked, walking into the foyer. When he got to the family room he practically swallowed his tongue. Rebecca lay on the couch in nothing but a frilly white apron with a chocolate cake in front of her on the coffee table.

She sat up and looked up at him.

"First, I want to say I'm sorry for offering to feed the vampire. I didn't know what it meant. I thought I was offering him a sandwich. I don't deliberately go looking for trouble." Aleks opened his mouth to speak but she held up a hand.

"Second, I'm sorry I'm not a bear shifter and can't be with you when your bear needs to get out. But I promise to always be waiting for you when you come home. Third, I know that a human marriage is nothing like a shifter claiming, but it does mean something to me. Sometime, whenever you're ready, I would like to get married." She hurried up with that request and looked down at the cake on the table, then back up at him. "I made you 'I'm sorry' cakes," she said, smiling timorously.

For as long as Aleks lived, he would never forget this moment. Her innocent apologies made naked in an apron. She could have asked for anything and he would have gladly done it. Did she have no idea how precious she was to him? He cleared his throat and removed his coat, throwing it on the chair.

"First, I want to apologize for not explaining about our world, including vampires. It left you vulnerable and it's my fault. I will take the time to tell you what you need to know. I know you don't go looking for trouble, but the fact that you are in danger makes me lose my mind. Please be patient with me." He took a step forward and removed his boots.

"Second, I want to apologize for losing my temper and making you feel like you are lacking as my mate. If given the choice between a huge furry body to sleep next to after shifting or coming home to my soft-skinned mate in nothing but an apron with cakes, I will choose you and the cakes every time," he said, then winked. He dug in the shirt pocket, removed the ring, but kept it hidden from her before removing the shirt and tossing it next to his boots.

"Third, I was an asshole to demean a human marriage, I should have known it meant something to you. I wouldn't have hurt you for the world." He removed his pants and let his heavy cock spring free. She licked her lips and he almost came. He stepped forward until he was standing in front of her then he knelt between her and the coffee table. He spread her legs and pulled her body forward until his cock lay nestled between her soft folds. They both sighed. Breathing heavily, he looked down at her half-closed eyes and smiled.

"In fact, I like the idea of something else tying us together. I went to my parents this morning and got this." He opened his hand and revealed a small ring with a large emerald set in the center.

"My grandfather had to leave town often to do business. My grandmother wanted him to have evidence that he was taken. They exchanged mating rings. This was hers. Would you do me the honor of becoming my wife?" he asked. He looked down and watched as tears began to run down her face.

"I love you so much! Yes! I will!" He slipped the ring on her finger and leaned down and kissed her, taking time to nibble her lips and plunge his tongue into her mouth over and over again. His eyes crossed when she reached down and grabbed his cock. She guided him to her entrance and thrust her hips upwards, taking him completely inside of her.

"As much as I would love to make love to you slowly right now, I can't. It's going to be fast and hard, baby," he said.

"I need you. Don't stop, this is perfect!" She arched her back. He lifted her hips a bit more until he was hitting that elusive spot inside of her on every stroke.

"No one, no one but me, you are mine!" he growled and slammed in her again.

"Only yours! Forever! If you stop, I swear I'm going to kill you in your sleep," she yelled. He grinned and pushed into her, picking up speed.

"God, I love the way you fuck me!" she said. His eyes went wide at her words, and he yelled, filling her with his seed. She screamed her release and deliberately squeezed him, milking every drop.

Aleks felt drained, so he pulled her down with him onto the floor between the couch and the coffee table. Panting and out of breath, he looked at her in wonder.

"Where did that come from?" he asked. She giggled.

"Rian suggested some dirty talk to spice things up. Did it work?" She looked at him, smiling.

"As if you have to ask," he said, snuggling her under his chin. She wrapped around him.

"You didn't even eat any cake, and I spent a lot of time last night making them for you," she said, yawning.

"What kind of cake?" he asked, perking back up. She laughed as he untied the apron and threw it across the room

"There is chocolate down here in the family room, coconut cake in the study, cinnamon rolls in the kitchen, your honey bun cake in the master bedroom, and vanilla jasmine pudding parfaits in the bathroom. It was a full out assault." She kissed his chest.

He reached up and ran his fingers through the chocolate icing before pushing them both to sitting positions with her straddling him. He began to paint her breasts in chocolate. He leaned forward and licked the icing away. She sighed as he wrapped his tongue around her nipple, tugging lightly before placing a small bite on the soft flesh. She gasped.

"So you wanted to spice things up?" he asked, placing another love bite on the side of her breast.

"Yes, I want to experience everything with you," she said, running her hands over his hair.

"Do you trust me, baby?" he asked.

"Of course I do," she said, looking up at him. "For a bear you have a decidedly wolfish grin."

"Get on all fours, baby," he said. He heard her heart begin to pound in her chest with excitement. She quickly complied. He ran his hand over one ass cheek then the other. She let out the breath she had been holding. His hand reached between her legs to find she was dripping moisture down her thigh. His eyes widened in surprise.

"Does my baby like the idea of being spanked?" he asked, popping her on her left cheek. A loud moan escaped her. Embarrassed at her reaction, she looked back at him, biting her lip.

"There's no reason to be embarrassed by anything we do, baby. Though it does earn you another smack." He hit her left cheek again.

"Put your hands over your head and don't move, baby." He leaned forward and kissed down her spine.

"Have you ever heard of using a safe word?" he asked.

"Yes," she said, shivering.

"What would you like as a safe word, baby?" he asked, nipping her shoulder blade.

"Cake," she said brightly. He smiled.

"If I do something that you don't like, cake is your safe word. Do you understand?" he asked.

"Yes, please do something," she begged.

"That earns you another five smacks. I give the orders, baby." In quick succession he smacked both left and right cheeks. They were starting to turn pink for him. He picked up the chocolate cake and dipped his fingers into the cake before smearing it on to her back. She gasped. Slowly he let his tongue caress her back as he licked every inch of her clean. She was moaning and squirming beneath him.

He reached under her to test her readiness to discover she was completely drenched. He reached down and lined up his cock with her entrance. He slammed his way home.

"Yes!" she screamed, and he smiled. He would go over not making noise later. He was enjoying it too much now.

"Count them off, baby." He plunged into her again before smacking her hard. He followed up with nine shallow strokes. She was clenching him tightly making him work hard to slam all the way home.

"One!" she screamed. He thrust into her twice more as deep as he could get and popped her on each ass cheek, followed by eight shallow strokes. Using her own juices he massaged her dark rosette and pushed a thumb in watching as it sucked the digit in. She gasped and pushed back wanting more.

"Two!" she yelled. He snapped his hips forward three times, alternated a slap on each ass cheek, and gave her seven shallow strokes.

"Does my baby like me playing in her tight ass? Do you want your dark hole filled too, baby?" Aleks asked.

"Three! Oh God yes!" she yelled. He wrapped off more hits and plunged his finger deep into her ass pushing down on the membrane as he felt his cock fill her up.

She lost track of counting when they hit six. She lost her voice when they hit eight, and her arms gave out at nine. When he slammed home ten times, alternating each thrust with a slap to her over-sensitized ass, she detonated. He roared his release as he kept coming. He had held back and made it to ten. Now his cum was dribbling back out of her and dripping down her legs. She collapsed completely. He had never come so hard in his life. He felt like his dick would fall off. With shaking arms, he reached up on the sofa and pulled down the throw he kept there. He wrapped her up and held her close. He kept whispering to her how much he loved her and how there was no one in the whole world for him but her.

"I loved your chocolate cake, baby. I can't wait to taste and experience them all." He grinned.

"Oh God," she gasped.

"It's Aleks, but close enough."

CHAPTER FOURTEEN

"**L**ET'S GO TO THAT CLUB to celebrate!" Rebecca said that afternoon when they were eating a late lunch at the diner. She kept squirming around on the barstool, the ache on her ass sent spirals of pleasure straight to her clit. She wiggled until she got comfortable trying to ignore her arousal. Aleks smiled knowing he had marked her in a way.

"Just because you know more about our world doesn't mean I'm going to take you clubbing."

She pouted then sniffled. "Please?"

Aleks groaned. She knew he wanted to keep her under lock and key wrapped in bubble wrap, preferably naked with cake.

"Aleks, we can't hide away in town. It will be like they are dictating ours lives. Please, please can we go to the club? I want to get out and dance and celebrate being mated to you," she said, looking up, her eyes pleading.

He sighed and turned his head to where Bran and Kate sat.

"Don't ask us to go. Clubs aren't my thing," Bran

said. Kate jabbed him in the ribs.

"As her maid of honor, I have to be there to celebrate. We're in!" Kate said.

Rebecca hid a grin. She loved Kate and Bran's dynamics.

"You're going to play up this maid of honor thing to the hilt, aren't you?" Bran said, shaking his head.

"I've never been in a wedding. This is going to be the social event of the decade. You better believe I'm milking this for all its worth," Kate said in a huff.

"At least until your wedding, right Kate?" Rebecca said evilly. Bran got a panicked look on his face. Kate winked at Rebecca.

"Okay, I found the perfect invitations!" Rian said, breezing through the diner's door with Damian and Liam.

"Hello, kitten, I hear you have trapped yourself a grouchy bear," Liam said, kissing Rebecca on the cheek, earning him a growl from Aleks. She grinned and kissed Liam in return.

"Why are you looking at invitations?" Aleks asked Rian, sounding confused.

"Rian and Damian are my wedding coordinators," Rebecca said, biting into her sandwich.

"Kate is my maid of honor and Ashby and Nicholas are my bridesmen," Rebecca said, grinning.

"Bridesmen? I didn't know you were that close to Ashby and Nicholas," he said.

"I did the neck thingy with them and now we're kinda linked. I think that definitely ranks them up there with best friend," she said, digging into her potato salad.

Aleks nodded then stopped. "What neck thing? You mean the submissive head tilt?" he asked.

"From time to time, when certain individuals pledge themselves to an Alpha Mother, they become more than part of the pack, pride, or sloth, they become part of what is called an Inner Court," Leona explained as she walked in with Ashby and Nicholas.

"Ma doesn't have one," Aleks said, frowning. Leona laughed and smiled at him.

"My dear boy, your mother is a force unto herself. Can you imagine her being comfortable sharing her emotions?" Leona asked, grinning. Both Aleks and Connor shook their heads fervently.

"Having an Inner Court doesn't denote strength or weakness. Sometimes we have gone hundreds of years without one. Each Inner Court is also different. In one case I read the Alpha Mother turned out to be a gentle-born lady used to court life. When she started meeting the townspeople, the artists, sculptors, and musicians were drawn to her. Her Inner Court provided what she would have lacked. Without music and art she would have been miserable and a terrible Alpha Mother. As a result Arkadia experienced a micro renaissance era. It was a very beautiful time in our history. In another documented case, the Prides and Packs were at war, which ended up drawing Arkadia into the fighting. When that Alpha Mother started meeting the townspeople, the warriors of the town were drawn to her. Her Inner Court became her body guards. They saved her life on seven occasions, once each time she was pregnant with the next generation.

"It all depends on the Alpha Mother or the situations they find themselves in when they take over. Even if the person pledges themselves to the Alpha, unless the need is there a bond doesn't form. It's a very good start to your time as Alpha Mother for you to have two already pledged and accepted." Leona sat at the table next to Kate and Bran. Everyone was staring at Rebecca, who started eating her chocolate pie. She looked up.

"What?" she asked. "If you think I'm some kind of super Alpha Mother thing, you're wrong. Ashby and Nicholas are just really great friends and we're tuned into one another," Rebecca said stubbornly.

"A ruling pair is an Alpha Mother and her Alpha, who acts as the enforcer." Everyone looked at Aleks.

"Ashby and Nicholas will guide you on the pulse of the town. They are in positions to speak to a lot of the townspeople." Everyone swung to stare at Ashby and Nicholas, who were blushing.

"You also have Liam and Kate, who have subconsciously taken on the roles of protectors," she said. Everyone stared at Liam and Kate. They shot looks to each other. Leona smiled slyly as if she had a secret before continuing.

"You already have a well-balanced support group, even if you don't form any other bonds," she said, sipping her coffee. Everyone looked around.

"Leona, where did you find all this information?" Rebecca asked when she couldn't bear the silence anymore.

"It's in the town archives," Leona said. Rebecca's eyes lit up. She loved diving into history.

"This could explain why the hyenas have been trying to get to her. They hate us. She represents our future and they know that," Connor said quietly.

"The attacks started after she claimed Ashby at the ice cream parlor before the hyenas were banned. I think one of them saw Ashby's claiming," Liam said.

"Why would they want me though? What does it gain them to take me?" Rebecca asked.

"Leverage. Aleks would move heaven and hell to get you back. He would also have the support of the pride and pack. They could ask for anything," Leona said.

"I didn't know they were that organized. The way you describe them, it makes them sound like backwoods rednecks that run meth labs at the edge of their properties. I wonder what they want that makes them so desperate that they would risk pissing Aleks off," Rebecca said, snuggling closer to him. He wrapped his arms around her.

"She's right, hyenas aren't known for being organized or intelligent or literate for that matter. They would usually piss themselves at the thought of going against Aleks. They must want something badly," Liam added.

"Or they found something that scares them more," Rebecca said quietly.

"Aleks, the next time you see a hyena, try not to maul it to death so we can ask it a few questions," Connor said with a grin.

"Yeah, Aleks," Liam said, chiming in. Aleks laughed.

"Like you're any better? I think the hyena that tried to grab Rebecca still hasn't made it to his car." He grinned and they bumped fists. Rebecca looked at them shocked.

"You like each other," she said matter-of-factly. Both men jumped back as if shocked.

"Bullshit," Aleks said.

"Never happen," Liam countered.

"Awww. You two are so cute! I was worried that you really didn't like each other. I felt bad because Liam takes such good care of me. But now I see that you're best friends," she said and then continued eating her pie. When she looked up at her mate he was staring down at her in horror, as if she just admitted to being pregnant with the Antichrist.

Bran lost all sense of composure and began to laugh and loudly. Kate joined in. Connor smiled and also began laughing.

"Busted," Emmett added from a table by the wall.

"Whatever," Aleks grumbled.

"So what time are we going to the club?" Rebecca asked and Aleks groaned.

"Club? What club?" Rian perked up.

"Aleks is taking me to that paranormal-only club in the flyer that the vampire gave me," Rebecca said, swinging around to face Rian. He and Damian exchanged glances.

"Whooooooo hoooooooooo!" Rian shouted and pulled Rebecca off her chair and out of Aleks' arms. They began to dance and grind in the middle of the diner. Kate jumped up and began to dance behind Rian, slapping him on the ass. Rian laughed and gyrated between the two females. Aleks and Bran growled lowly, and both women ignored them.

"Is it just me or does it feel like this town is

coming to life with Rebecca here?" Pa asked Ma as they walked out of her office.

Aleks pulled Rebecca away from Rian and Kate. Rebecca laughed as Aleks' face turned bright red from Rian popping him on the ass. Rian then ran behind Kate. Both Kate and Rebecca dissolved into giggles.

"Because it has. This town has always been a safe haven for shifters. But she is making it a home," Ma said before clearing her throat, everyone turned to face her. "My time may be coming to an end as Alpha Mother, but I'm going to do everything in my power to hand over Arkadia during a happy and peaceful time." She eyed Aleks. "That being said, maybe going to the club isn't such a bad idea," she started, and Aleks opened his mouth as if to say something. She held up a hand. He closed his mouth and waited.

"I just got off the phone with Elder Lachlan..." Liam hissed, interrupting her.

Rebecca looked at him in fascination. "Who is Elder Lachlan?" she asked, curiously.

"The Lion Elder who rules all the cats," Ma replied.

"A meddlesome old bastard," Liam said at the same time, and Ma rolled her eyes.

"Language, Liam! And you shouldn't speak of your grandfather like that. He does care a great deal about you," she said, and he gave a cynical bark of laughter.

"The only thing that old man is concerned about is his council seat, which I don't want by the way," he said.

"He thinks you would be a wonderful Elder,

but that is neither here nor there." She turned to Rebecca. "The vampire you met in the bookstore. Can you describe him?"

Rebecca sighed, smiling. Aleks growled.

"He was tall, shoulder-length wavy black hair, strong jaw, perfect smile, and the most brilliant blue eyes I have ever seen," she recounted. Rian, Damian, Ashby, and Kate sighed. Bran and Aleks scowled. Ma hid a smile.

"Did he have any other distinguishing features?" she asked.

"His eyes changed color. He had red glowy eyes at first, scary but cool. Then they changed to teal then a royal blue. He also had the coolest antique ring I've ever seen," she said.

"The eyes changing color and the signet ring confirms it." Ma pinched the bridge of her nose.

"Ma? What is it?" Aleks asked.

"Rebecca, did he seem pleasant?" Ma waited for Rebecca's reply.

"Yes, he was extremely polite. He kissed my hand and said it was a 'distinct pleasure' to meet me. He liked me," she said.

Ma smiled at Rebecca as Aleks started growling lowly and began to kiss each hand as if to remove the vampire's touch.

"Everyone likes you, baby girl. It seems to be your gift. One that, I think, might have saved us," she said. Aleks looked up from Rebecca's hands.

"Ma, you're really starting to scare me. What is going on?"

Ma looked at her. "Rebecca, the man that you by happenstance ran into at the bookstore and unknowingly charmed, was none other than

Prince Gabriel, leader of all vampires, and is said to be one of the coldest men of his race." Aleks looked from his Ma to Rebecca, to Ma, and then back to Rebecca. He grabbed Rebecca, putting her in his lap, wrapped his arms around her, and placed his chin on her head. Rebecca, feeling his fear, began to rub her hands up and down his forearms soothingly.

"I'm sorry, I thought you said Prince Gabriel. Ma, that can't be right. He is known to be ruthless, cold, calculating, and he never leaves his coven," Bran said, grabbing Kate and holding her close.

Ma shook her head. "Elder Lachlan reported that the council has been tracking his movements over the past year. He has evidently moved his coven to the town outside of Arkadia and opened a paranormal-only club called Purgatory."

"Fuck!" Liam exploded.

"Normally I would say something about your language, Liam, but that sums it up nicely. Fuck indeed," Ma said, and everyone just stared at her. For her to be cussing said volumes.

"This is so cool! I think Purgatory is a wicked name for a club. I can't wait to go now," Rebecca exploded.

Everyone as one turned and stared at her.

"What? Until he proves otherwise, Gabriel is a good guy in my book. His actions were that of a perfect gentleman. You can't always believe what people say," she said pointedly.

Everyone was quiet, lost in their own thoughts.

"You're absolutely right, Rebecca. I have always been afraid of others based on what I believed of them to be true. I am ashamed I let so much time go by without reaching out and missed years of friendship," Ashby said, smiling at Rian and Damian, who grinned back in return.

"You have been chosen to be our next Alpha Mother for a reason. We'll follow your lead on this," Kate said, looking around the room.

"And if that person or persons proves to be dangerous or breaks their trust with you..." Bran said, looking at Aleks and Liam, who nodded.

"*Then* we destroy them," Liam said simply.

"Great! Now that we have our world domination plans settled," Rebecca grinned. "Let's call and arrange a meeting at this wickedly named club. Then we can party!" she said, bouncing up and down on Aleks's lap. He grimaced and stilled her bouncing. She looked back over her shoulder and up at him, then bounced twice more before wiggling to get comfortable. She could feel Aleks's semi erect cock spring to life. Aleks groaned as his head fell backwards. His lips were moving and Rebecca heard him faintly counting to ten. Connor and Rian started making catcalls. Rebecca blushed and started laughing.

"I'll call and make arrangements," Ma said, covering her mouth to hide her smile.

CHAPTER FIFTEEN

"ALEKS, THE LINE STARTS BACK there," Rebecca said, pointing to the end of the long line that was starting to snake around the corner. Rebecca smiled nervously at the people who were staring at them. But she had to admit their group made an impressive sight. All seven Arkadion brothers, Kate, Bran, Liam, Rian, Damian, Ashby, and Nicholas were all sporting their best club wear.

The Arkadion brothers seemed to have gone with a leather theme. They were decked out in leather pants and different color silk shirts. They had on boots that screamed "bad ass biker" and leather jackets to keep out the worst of the winter's cold. She knew they had to have bikes somewhere. After seeing them together like this she was going to make them take her riding when the weather turned. She looked at all the leather. *Yummy*. Her eyes went to Bran and Kate, they looked like they just walked out of a high society magazine. Bran was rocking a grey suit with no tie, and Kate was pulling some serious lust-filled stares with her backless red, skin-tight dress. Ashby and Nicholas complimented each other, wearing jeans and flashy club tops, and Liam surprised her when he showed up wearing jeans, a white button-down with the sleeves rolled up onto his thick forearms, and a large belt buckle. *Take me away, cowboy.* Whenever Aleks wasn't looking, she kept staring at the Arkadion men standing together. She sighed. He looked down, his eyes narrowed. She just grinned up at him.

"You keep checking them out and Aleks will put you over his knee," Kate said, smiling.

"That's what I'm hoping." Rebecca winked and Kate laughed.

Aleks walked right up to the two vampires who were watching the door. They watched him approach.

"Sir, the line forms back there," the blond vampire said without batting an eye. Aleks just stared at him, his face grim. The blond stared back. After another moment, the blond started to look nervous.

"Name?" he asked.

"Aleksander Arkadion," Aleks responded. The vampire's eyes widened and he stood straighter.

"My apologies, sir, please come this way. I will show you and your party to our VIP section," the blond replied, pushing back the line of waiting guests to open the double doors so that their group could enter. His hands shook as he lifted the clasp to the velvet rope to clear the path. Once the rope was lifted Liam led the way and their group started to head into the club.

"Do you know if Gabriel is here yet?" Rebecca

asked. Aleks looked down at her, surprised at her question and the blond vampire's eyes widened and a flash of unease crossed his features.

"Oh God, you know the Prince. I am so sorry to have kept you waiting," he replied. Rebecca reached forward and patted him on the arm. Aleks stood off to one side waiting for her.

"I only met him the one time when he invited us to come see his club. Don't worry, I think you're doing a great job at making sure the club is secure," she said, smiling. The blond relaxed a fraction.

"Thank you, Ms....?" he asked.

"I'm Rebecca Morgan, but soon I'll be Rebecca Arkadion," she said, showing him her ring excitedly. The blond gave her a gentle smile. Aleks rolled his eyes.

"Congratulations to you both. I'll make sure a bottle of our finest champagne is sent to your table to celebrate your mating," the blond vampire replied.

"Thank you... What is your name?" she asked.

"I'm Bryn, and this is Radek," Bryn said, pointing to the dark-haired vampire holding the door open for the pair. Radek waved.

"It's nice to meet you both," Rebecca said as Aleks took her hand and led her past the door.

Once inside, they had to walk through another set of heavy glass doors to get to the heart of the club. When Aleks swung the glass door open the bass of the music moved through Rebecca's body. She felt an instinctive need to dance and move.

"Come on!" she yelled and pointed up to the balcony where she could see Rian and Damian already moving to the music. The VIP section overlooked the dance floor. Aleks smiled and nodded. The crowd seemed to part as he walked through a throng of people to head to the stairs leading to the balcony.

Rebecca found herself wanting to imitate Liam and hiss at the women who were openly checking out her mate. She was starting to understand his need to be constantly touching her. At the top of the stairs the room to the right opened up as the large VIP lounge which had a long elegant table with chairs. There were soft-looking leather sofas that lined the wall to the left which was directly across from the balcony rail. Rebecca smiled and headed to where Kate and Rian stood at the railing, looking down. The balcony was closed off floor to ceiling with a thick clear glass, leaving a panel in the middle open. It left whoever was in the balcony able to talk to their guests, still hear the music, and feel like they were in the middle of the action. Rebecca had to admit it was extremely impressive.

Kate turned and grabbed her in a hug. "I'm so glad we came. Bran and I wouldn't have warranted this kind of treatment if we came alone." She grinned at Bran, who rolled his eyes.

"What took you so long in getting up here?" Kate asked.

"The blond vampire, whose name I found out is Bryn, looked scared that we were mad about being kept waiting. When I mentioned Gabriel's name, he looked like he wanted to cry, so I tried to make him feel better. He really was doing a great job. He and Radek, the dark-haired vampire, probably thought we were just trying to cut the line," she said in almost one breath.

Aleks shook his head. "No matter how many times I hear them, I love your cute rambles."

Rebecca smiled. "That's good because you're stuck with me."

And the sooner I can let those heifers down there know it the better.

When the first few bars from "Wobble" started playing, Rian, Ashby, Damian, Rebecca, and Kate yelled and dashed for the steps to make it down to the dance floor. Nicholas and the others laughed and watched them from the balcony. Aleks eyes followed Rebecca as she moved from side to side swaying her body to the music. He found himself smiling when she smiled and straining to hear her laughter. When she rotated her hips, he growled and his pants seemed to grow just a bit tighter.

He turned when an auburn-haired vampire appeared at the door. "Sir, Prince Gabriel will see you now," he said.

Aleks had to grind his teeth. The way it was said made him feel like a subject being summoned. Liam placed a hand on his shoulder. Aleks looked at him, from the sour expressions on his and Bran's faces he could tell they felt the same.

They were led to an office on the third floor. The man stopped and knocked on the door twice, before swinging it open and ushering them inside. Behind the ebony desk sat an extremely pale and extraordinarily handsome man. Aleks stepped forward and inclined his head in greeting. The man raised an eyebrow before indicating to the black leather chairs. The three men sat down.

"That will be all, Noel," Gabriel said. Noel bowed and left the room.

"Bran McGregor, mated to Kate Edwards. Alpha of the Arkadian wolf pack. Fought and killed your father to take the title of Alpha twenty years ago and have been having trouble with pack members with the arrival of your mate Kate," Gabriel said as he read from a folder. He tossed it down and picked up the next.

"Liam Lewenhart, unmated. Alpha of the Arkadian lion pride. There seemed to be an issue with your views on sexual orientation. When you were successful in the dominance fight with your Father, the entire elder generation left, rather than have you as Alpha. The Arkadion Alpha Mother however supported you. You opened up your pride to those who had been kicked out of their own prides for being gay. You run a pride comprised solely of males." He raised a single brow at Liam and set the folder down.

"And finally Aleksander Arkadion. You are the eldest amongst your brothers, which makes you heir to the Alpha position. You served in an all-shifter unit in the Raleigh police force before returning home to take up position as sheriff. You recently mated one Rebecca Morgan. The first human I have met in many centuries with a nearly pure aura. I had the pleasure of meeting her in the bookshop." He set the last folder down, leaned back, and folded his hands in front of him.

"You seem to know us pretty well," Bran said in a tight voice.

"Those are only the bare essentials. The other folders have your bank information, blood type, and what you ate for breakfast this morning," he said, taking time to look each of them in the eye. "What I don't know is why you requested a meeting with me," he said.

"Why did you move your coven so close to Arkadia?" Aleks started.

"I don't see how I have to explain anything to you," Gabriel said coldly.

"I don't like unknowns. I'm having too many problems with the damn hyenas who decided to go bat-shit crazy out of nowhere," Aleks said heatedly.

Gabriel sat forward. "You either are completely oblivious to what has been going on or a damn good actor," he said.

"You obviously know something we don't. If it pertains to the hyenas or why they have been going after Rebecca, you need to tell me. Or you can keep acting like an asshole and I get to beat it out of you," Aleks said grimly. Bran groaned and Liam smacked his forehead with his hand.

Gabriel's mouth twitched. "It's kind of cute that you think you can take me. Your attitude tells me a lot about you. So does your aura. Right now it's telling me you are very closely synced with your bear so that in instances where perhaps diplomacy might work better you make honest threats. I actually respect that more than deceit. It's also telling me that you love your mate with everything in you. That is rare, but having met Rebecca I can

understand." He stood and walked over to a sim-
ulated window that was actually an LED monitor
showing different rooms of the club.

"I had to make sure you weren't involved. I apologize for the lightly veiled insults," he said, turning
around. The cold mask had slipped away, leaving
him looking tired. Bran and Liam sat forward. If the
powerful man before them was stressed over whatever was happening, they were utterly screwed.

"I take it these vague statements will eventually
end and you can tell us what the fuck is going
on," Aleks said.

Gabriel's eyes widened slightly. "You are as
refreshing and honest as Rebecca, just in completely different ways," he said. "Without any vague
statements, we're fucked, gentleman." He walked
back over to his desk and sat down.

"Well shit," Liam said, sitting back.

"I hate to tell you, but that's still vague," Aleks
said sarcastically.

Gabriel reached into his desk and pulled out a
stack of photos. "About eighteen months ago I
was called to a coven in Detroit to settle a dispute
between two houses. One vampire murdered the
other vampire's daughter in a fit of rage. Around
the same time the local wolf pack reported two
missing families to your council. Two weeks after
that incident I was called to New York. One vampire beat to death, then ripped the head off another
vampire who argued with him over who was
going to win the Super Bowl. In that instance an
entire shifter-only fraternity went missing. Three
weeks after that I was contacted by a coven leader
in Boston. After a group of vampires went through

town, a small, local, lion family was gone. Not dead, gone. It probably would have gone unnoticed if the coven leader wasn't good friends with the lion family. We haven't found the bodies. Seeing a pattern yet?" he said, putting the pictures of the missing and the deceased on the table.

"Vampires are flipping out and shifters are going missing." Liam's face went extremely pale. "Someone is distributing shifter blood to vampires." Liam whispered, as if saying it quieter would make it less true.

"That is impossible. Vampires feeding off of shifter blood is forbidden, it's the oldest law between both our peoples, one of the first created, punishable by death. Everyone knows that shifter blood is dangerous to vampires. The effects are unpredictable," Aleks argued.

"It's out there, gentleman, being bought and sold like a designer drug," Gabriel confirmed.

"How do the hyenas tie into all of this?" Aleks asked, afraid he knew where it was going.

"From what I can piece together from the few unlucky runners and dealers I have been able to catch, is that this all started with a gambling debt. A hyena owed and owed big. When the vampires went to collect, he offered up his blood as payment, saying it would give them a great buzz. The idiot vampires believed him. Soon he wasn't enough, so the hyena, seeing a business opportunity, offered to start bringing in unsuspecting shifters for their blood. That was about a two years ago, and business is doing well," Gabriel said.

"Hyenas aren't that smart," Liam said, standing. He started to pace. Aleks could tell that Liam's lion wanted to hunt.

"You're right, they aren't, but the vampires are. They already had connections with all the wrong people. They are using the hyenas as suppliers," Gabriel said.

"Why go after Rebecca?" Aleks asked.

"I tracked the clan of hyenas who are the main suppliers to just outside of Arkadia. Two weeks ago they fucked up and lost a huge shipment of blood that was set to go north. It would be my guess that they would use Rebecca to get you to drain Arkadia dry to make up for that loss. They will only be getting more desperate. I bet they are on a timeline," Gabriel said. He pushed forward one eight-by-ten black-and-white photo. "Does he look familiar?"

Aleks looked down and nodded. "That's the hyena Rebecca and I saw the night at the restaurant." He handed the picture to Bran.

Liam walked over from where he had been staring at the LED monitor. "I just saw that guy in the club!" he said, taking the picture.

Bran gasped. "Something is wrong. Can you see Kate?" Bran demanded, clutching his midsection.

Aleks was about to stand when a blinding pain to the back of his head nearly made him pass out. He stood and staggered, struggling to remain upright. "Where is Rebecca?" he asked going to the monitors.

"Liam, are you sure?" Gabriel asked as he strode over to stand next to Aleks. He pushed aside the dark wood paneling to reveal a wall of monitors. He started scanning each screen.

"Wolves and bears are good with scents. Lions

are good with details and tracking. I'm one of the best when it comes to hunting. That and I thoroughly beat the shit out of that guy in Arkadia, I wouldn't forget something like that" Liam said, joining him at the wall.

Outside they heard raised voices.

"I don't care! I need to talk to him. Aleks! Aleks!" a voice yelled from the other side of the door. Gabriel beat Aleks to the door and flung it open to reveal a crying Nicholas, who was clutching his chest.

"Nicholas, what is it?" Aleks asked, fear knotting in his throat.

"I felt panic, then pain from Ashby. Then panic, then anger, then pain from Rebecca, and then nothing. I don't feel them anymore!" he wailed.

Aleks roared and the walls shook. People stopped talking and the music cut so quickly the last notes echoed through the building.

He ran past Nicholas and down the stairs, Liam and Bran steps behind him. He saw Connor talking to Rian and Damian, who were shaking their heads and crying. They looked up as Aleks approached at a run.

"Bathroom," Connor said, taking off at a run to the side hallway, the men following him. When they got there, Emmett, Benedict, and Duncan were questioning people in the bathroom hallway as Gavin treated Kate, who lay motionless on the floor.

"Where is she?" Aleks roared. His hands became claws, and he raked them down the walls, sending wood and plaster flying.

"Kate!" Bran yelled, falling to his knees beside

his mate.

"Rebecca and Ashby were taken out the emergency exit by four hyenas. Kate was trying to stop them when they stabbed her in the stomach. I don't have any supplies here, Aleks," Gavin said urgently, his hands full of blood as he tried to staunch the bleeding.

"Noel, take this gentleman and Ms. Edwards to our clinic downstairs. Give them anything and everything they need. Radek, Bryn, I need to move any witnesses to the VIP section and clear out the rest. Aleks, who is your best tracker?" Gabriel asked, turning to Aleks, who stood beside them, chest heaving. "Aleks, I can't even pretend to know how hard this is for you, but you are the next leader of Arkadia. You need to focus," Gabriel said softly.

Aleks' head snapped to Gabriel. "Benedict and Finn, are our best trackers, Liam is our best hunter. I trust him to take charge out in the field," he said through clenched teeth. He was barely keeping himself from shifting. His bear was clawing at him to get out, to go get his mate. But the human side of him knew they had a better chance of getting her back if he could focus and start working this as a crime scene. He took a deep breath and looked at Gabriel.

"We need to isolate each witness and get statements." Gabriel nodded then moved to where Bryn was ushering the witnesses upstairs. He turned to his brother "Emmett, I need you to guard the scene. We can't have too many people down here. The scents we have are already fading. I don't want any gawkers trailing through them, destroying them completely."

Emmett nodded then simply started walking, arms stretched out, until each hand touched either side of the hallway and pushed everyone down the hallway using his body as a plunger before blocking the entrance.

"Connor, I need you to get Rian and Damian down here. The three of you will be looking for any kind of trace evidence." Connor nodded then ran past Emmett to go get the two lions.

Aleks turned to Duncan. "I need to you to call Ma, tell her everything that happened. Get Dr. Claybourne up here. You also need to call Riley and let him know that his Alphas need him and the pack," Aleks said, referring to Bran's Beta. Duncan nodded and pulled out his cell phone.

That only left Nicholas. Before Rebecca, he never would have thought of the smaller man. His eyes moved past the onlookers until he saw him on the outskirts of the crowd, his arms wrapped around his body and silent tears streaming down his face. He looked lost. Aleks walked past Emmett and walked over to Nicholas, who looked up at him, his face ashen.

"Alpha, I..." His voice broke.

"I need you to stay by my side, Nicholas. Besides our mating bond, you are my only tie to her. If you feel anything, anything at all, tell me right away," he said gently. He placed a hand on Nicholas's shoulder.

"Of course, Alpha, I'll do anything to get them back," he swore. Aleks nodded and looked up. Gabriel was motioning that they join him.

"Two witnesses said that they heard the hyenas say something about making a delivery. They should be contacting us soon," Gabriel informed him.

"I can't sacrifice Arkadia," Aleks said.

"No one said you should. Rebecca seems the kind of woman who wouldn't want others hurt for her sake. We'll find them, Aleks. Then we'll take out these hyenas, and the vampire's blood supply will dry up," Gabriel said lowly.

"What happens to the vampires?" Aleks asked, looking at Gabriel. He was surprised when the vampires eyes started to glow a dim red color.

"They face me," Gabriel said coldly. Aleks nodded. He would have preferred to rip them apart with his bare hands, but one look at Gabriel's eyes and Aleks knew that killing them would be a mercy. He wanted them to suffer, so they would be facing their Prince.

CHAPTER SIXTEEN

"EWW, IT SMELLS LIKE SHIT in here, I mean like, literal shit," Rebecca said, shifting her body so that she lay on her side facing Ashby. They had both woken up with their hands tied behind their backs.

"I'll take your word for it. That jerk broke my nose," Ashby said, wincing as he spoke.

"Not to sound ungrateful, because if you weren't here I'd be losing my mind, but why did they bring you?" Rebecca asked.

Ashby gave a small chuckle. "Because they couldn't separate us. Even when they knocked us unconscious we didn't let go of each other," he said, giving her a soft smile.

"Aww, I wuve you too, Ashers," Rebecca said, making a kissy face.

He laughed then gasped. "I think they broke a few ribs too," he said, breathing out slowly. Rebecca growled and Ashby grinned. "You know, they say that after a while couples start acting alike. That is the tiniest growl I have ever heard, and I babysit," he said, grinning. Rebecca laughed.

"So, what's the plan?" she asked. Ashby was about to respond when the door to the room they were in slid open. When light filled their room, Rebecca realized she wasn't in a building at all, it looked like they were in a railcar.

"Quiet in there, no talking or we beat the tiny lion some more," a harsh voice called, before slamming the door closed.

"Why does he think you're a lion?" she whispered as low as she could.

"At the club I was dancing between Rian and Damian. It must be their sweat. It explains why I'm tied up and not in a cage. If they knew I could shift smaller and out of my bonds I'd be in a cage," he explained.

"Then shift, go!" she whispered.

"Never going to happen, Rebecca, I will never leave my Alpha Mother," he said.

"Look, I appreciate the sentiment. But if Aleks, Liam and Bran knew where we were, those hyenas would be in tiny pieces by now. We were out for a while, so there's no telling how far we are from the club. We're in a railcar. We're both covered in coal dust. Railcars move, Ashby. They could move us anywhere in the mine. We're stationary now, but God only knows if that will change. They would never find us. I mean who starts looking in railcars? They will probably mount an army and storm the woods. Shift, go get help. Even if they move the railcar, at least you could let them know to look for one," she whispered. She knew it would be a long shot, but at least he would be safe if he left.

"I can't leave you alone. You're human, they'll kill you," Ashby replied, tears in his eyes. She scooted forward and kissed his forehead.

"If they wanted us dead, we'd be dead. They need me to control Aleks. Ashby, I am asking you to leave me here and go get help." She looked him in the eye. "Please."

He looked at her for a long moment, then nodded. He closed his eyes, and his human form disappeared and he shrunk down to a tiny white fox. She smiled when he raced behind her and started chewing through the bonds. When they snapped apart, he went to where she was lying and licked her face.

She giggled. "Thank you for freeing my hands. They were starting to hurt." She ran a hand over his soft fur.

"Go!" she whispered. He ran for the corner of the railcar where the metal had rusted out leaving a small hole. He wiggled through and then, he was gone.

Aleks was standing in front of the club in the empty parking lot watching the sun come up. His Ma and Pa had arrived in the night with Riley, some of Bran's wolves, a few of Liam's lions and Dr. Claybourne. Purgatory became their base of operations. His mouth twisted at the irony. He felt like he was in Purgatory, a limbo between Heaven and Hell. His head turned at the sound of quickly approaching feet.

"Aleks, they're on the phone," Connor said,

breathlessly. Aleks raced past him up the stairs to Gabriel's office. Gabriel stood next to his desk and motioned to the phone.

"Okay, he's here, say your piece, parasite," Gabriel said. A maniacal laugh floated through the room from the speaker phone.

"I want to hear the Arkadion, or, you get to hear his bitch." His voice stopped and a painful scream filled the room. Everyone jerked.

"Rebecca! You motherfucker! If you hurt her, I will fucking end you!" he screamed.

"I doubt you will get the chance. Here are my terms. You get me six pints of blood from every shifter in Arkadia. My men will pick it up at the town's entrance." He chuckled lowly. "Except for you. I want every drop of your blood, Aleksander Arkadion. My client will be extremely happy to get the young virile blood of the Arkadion King." The hyena cackled.

"No! Aleks, don't do it. Look to the east, Gandalf should be coming to rescue Gimli from the mines of Moria," she yelled. There were laughs, the sound of flesh hitting flesh, and another scream.

"Uh-oh, Arkadion, her mind is already cracking. You have until tomorrow morning." And then the line went dead.

Aleks roared. Ma stepped forward and wrapped her arms around her son.

"We'll get started in getting the blood," she said firmly.

"Aleks, you give them that blood and you'll never see her alive again. They will keep her and torture her just to keep you and Arkadia in a position to be blood whores," Gabriel said quietly.

"What do you suggest? I am not leaving my daughter in the hands of those insane monsters!" Ma retorted.

That snapped Aleks out of his rage. "We have to find her. He's right, if we give them blood now, they will just use her to drain the town dry. What do we know?" he asked, turning to Gabriel.

"Not much. We have the two witnesses who say they heard something about a delivery. Another bystander who says they smelled of metal, and another witness who refuses to leave the hallway until he identifies what is is smelling. He says it smells like dead plants and animals," Gabriel said, rubbing his bloodshot eyes.

Aleks had found out that Gabriel normally rested during the day. Most of the prince's men had gone underground to gather their strength, leaving only Gabriel and his acting second-in-command Roman awake.

"What was it that she said about Gandalf?" Duncan asked looking around the room.

"She said that Gandalf would be coming from the east to rescue Gimli," Emmett replied absently.

Out of nowhere Connor began to laugh. He laughed as he danced a jig around the office. Everyone stared. He turned and grabbed Aleks by the arms. "Aleks, your mate is a fucking genius!" he said.

"I know," Aleks said feeling confused.

"No! She is an authentic genius. She has an eidetic memory and she's a goddamn librarian! Do you really think she would misquote Tolkien?" he asked. Looking around the room, he got blank stares.

"Really! Come on, people, didn't you even watch the movies? Gandalf didn't ride in from the east to help Gimli," he said, waiting for them to put the pieces together.

"Gandalf the Grey didn't help Gimli, he helped the Rohirrim at Helm's Deep!" Duncan exclaimed.

"He wasn't Gandalf the Grey then, he was Gandalf the White, he kicked some major ass once he was white." Emmett said out of nowhere.

"White. She liked his pretty white fur," Aleks said, smiling.

"Fuck! I think we're losing him, people. Keep your shit together, man," Liam said, walking up to Aleks shaking him slightly.

"Ashby!" Aleks yelled.

"No, I'm Liam," he said cautiously.

"Not you, asshole. Ashby! Ashby is white, not grey. He will be heading from the east from a mine where Rebecca is being held! The shifter in the hallway can't place the scent. The smell of dead plants and animals must be coal! She's near a coal mine," Aleks said and grabbed Connor in a huge hug.

"My mate is a freaking genius!" he said, smiling for the first time in hours.

"Ashby!" Nicholas yelled, holding his phone up to his ear. Everyone got quiet and turned to Nicholas. Aleks ran over to stand beside him.

"Ashby, you're breaking up, where are you?" Nicholas screamed into his phone.

"Ashby! Ashby!" Nicholas looked at his phone in panic.

"All I heard was the word 'railcars'," he said, looking at the phone then up at the group.

"There have only been a few active mines in North Carolina, and all three are located about four hours east of here," Gabriel said.

"Nicholas, you're with me. Bring your phone. Let's go, people!" Aleks said, and everyone scrambled.

CHAPTER SEVENTEEN

"DAMN CELL PHONES!" ASHBY YELLED and threw the one he managed to steal into the woods. He was freezing his ass off with no clothes and not many options to get any. It was winter. It wasn't like people were hanging their clothes out on their clotheslines. He shifted back to his fox form.

He figured with his tiny legs it would take him two years to get to where Aleks and Nic were. Hoping that he gave them enough to find them, he headed back towards where Rebecca was being held. He didn't like leaving her alone. He would have better luck stealing another cell phone from one of the hyenas than trying to walk through two feet of snow when he was only ten inches tall.

It was late afternoon when they arrived in the county that held one of the abandoned mines. Nic was whimpering in the back seat. He had started shaking with cold about an hour ago, and Aleks took that as a good sign. It meant he was close enough to be sharing physical distress. Aleks was desperate to pick up something from Rebecca but got nothing. When Nic's shaking became almost uncontrollable Aleks pulled the car over signaling everyone to stop.

"He's getting closer. He's close," Nicholas said. Aleks jumped from the car and ran over to where Bran sat in the SUV with Liam.

Only Kate threatening to withhold sex if Bran didn't help look for Rebecca had gotten him to join the search party. He reluctantly left her side after getting Pa's promise to stay with her.

Aleks knew that Bran's wolf had to be howling for revenge. His own bear was no less blood-thirsty.

"Bran, Nic says that Ashby is close. Can you guys shift and sniff him out?" he asked. Bran nodded, and he and two of his men headed for the woods.

The wait was excruciating for Aleks. Finally after thirty minutes Bran appeared at the edge of the woods, a half-frozen white fox in his mouth. Being an alpha, Bran was nearly double in size compared to the other wolves, and it made Ashby look even smaller. Aleks ran forward and gently took Ashby from Bran's mouth. The wolf turned and headed back into the woods to where he left his clothes so he could shift back.

Aleks carried Ashby to the SUV and gently laid him beside Nicholas. After a few moments, the white fox disappeared and Ashby lay there naked and shivering. The bond they had with Rebecca and each other seemed to be different than a mating bond. The mating bond concentrated on feelings and emotions to better ensure open communication and giving your mate what they needed. This bond seemed to be more centered around protection and could be felt over greater distances. He quickly covered Ashby with a blanket as he and Nicholas lay huddled together. Dr.Claybourne lifted Ashby's wrist to check his pulse.

"Ashby, where is Rebecca?" he asked.

"I tried to call," Ashby said, shaking.

"I know, we got your phone call. It got us this far, but we need to know where she is," Aleks repeated, getting impatient. Doc scowled at him.

"I tried to make my way back to Rebecca, but I got lost. Everything looked the same from my height. I got turned around," Ashby said, teeth chattering.

"Can you get us there now?" Aleks asked. Ashby looked up and nodded.

"Head towards the old coal mine and then head east. It's an offshoot strip mining location. They have her in a railcar that's in the center of their camp," he said as his shaking subsided.

"Ashby, thank you!" Aleks said and jumped from the SUV. He got his brothers and the men organized. With any luck Rebecca would be in his arms before sunset.

They moved in at dusk. Aleks decided to stay in human form so that he could tend to Rebecca when she was found. He paced and waited for the signal. When they heard the screams of the dying hyenas who had been watching the perimeter, everyone began to move. Aleks charged forward. His goal was to get to the railcar as quickly as he could. If he had to rip apart the hyenas that stood between him and his mate, so be it.

Body after body was shredded by his claws. He didn't even see them as people, just objects in his way. He reached the railcar and threw the door open, snapping the chain that was holding it closed. It was empty. The smell of his mate filled the car. He could smell blood, a lot of his mate's blood, but the car was empty. He threw his head back and roared. Six roars echoed in response as his brothers shared in his frustration. He ran to where the fight was dying down. Bran had a man before him on his knees about to rip his throat out.

"Bran wait! Rebecca isn't here," Aleks yelled. Bran didn't stop his swing, only retracted his claws and pummeled the man into the ground.

"Where is she?" Aleks demanded. He lifted the man up with one hand and shook him.

"You'll never find her, Arkadion. She'll die and you'll never find her." The hyena screeched. Aleks looked around helplessly. She could be anywhere. He threw his head back again and roared.

"You may kill us, but your mate is beyond your reach. The rest of my clan will use her to get what we want!" The hyena cackled then coughed up blood causing it to dribble down his chin.

Aleks fought back waves of rage. Giving in to his anger wouldn't help him now, he had to think. He turned to Bran. "Search the woods! Anywhere they may have fled with her."

Bran nodded and started barking out orders.

"Search! Run! You'll never see your mate again," the hyena taunted.

Liam brought his fist down knocking the man unconscious. He looked over at him. "We're going to find her Aleks," he promised.

Aleks fought back his bear. He looked his closest friend. "God I hope so, for all our sakes," he whispered.

Liam's eyes widened at his declaration and the weight behind the statement hit home.

There would be no Aleks without Rebecca, and no Arkadia without the Arkadion and Alpha Mother. Their entire world hinged on one small human.

"I'm telling you, I feel like she's this way," Ashby said pulling on Nic's arm.

"Are you sure? I thought you said she was in a railcar?" Nic asked.

Ashby nodded. "She was, but now doesn't she feel like she's more over here?" He stopped walking and looked into the dark entrance of an ominous looking cave. Roars and screams sounded off all around them.

"You're right, it feels like my heart is tugging toward the cave," Nic agreed.

Ashby began to shake and it had nothing to do with the temperature. He hated dark closed in spaces.

Nic reached down and took his hand. "Come on, she needs us," Nic reminded him.

Ashby took a deep breath. There wasn't much he wouldn't do for his Alpha Mother.

Together they made their way down a steep incline. The further they descended the darker it got.

"Thank god foxes are nocturnal," Nic whispered.

Ashby walked close to his friend. "She has to be okay."

"She will be Ash. We'll make sure of it."

They walked for another five minutes before Ashby's nose began to burn. "Do you smell that?"

Nic had already covered his nose with his hand. "Is that ammonia?"

Ashby skidded to a halt. "Don't they use ammonia in morgues to cover up the smell of dead people?"

They looked at each other for a second then ran recklessly headlong into the darkness. "Rebecca!" Ashby yelled.

"Here!" a soft voice rasped weakly.

Ashby ran to the small figure huddled in the middle of the cavern. Rebecca was naked and lying on her stomach in a pool of ammonia. She had a shackle around her ankle and was chained to the floor.

"Oh god! Nic!" Ashby yelled dropping to his knees. Rebecca's back looked like raw hamburger. "We have to get her outta here and to Doc Claybourne."

Nic was already moving. He picked up the shackle and pulled it apart freeing her leg. He then stood looking around. In one corner a couple of old wooden crates were stacked to one side. Using his fist he punched one until it cracked open. He lifted out a wool blanket. "This will have to do."

"That was kinda sexy," Rebecca teased weakly.

Ashby forced a smile. He could tell Rebecca was holding on by a thread. "Let's get you up okay? Then we can go find Doc Claybourne, he can have you fixed up in a jiffy," he said brightly, though he felt his smile wobble.

"Liar," she whispered.

Ashby helped her to stand, letting her lean on him.

Nic gently wrapped the blanket around her, freezing when Rebecca hissed in pain. Tears were streaming down his cheeks. "I am so sorry," he choked out.

"Not...not your fault," she gasped.

They moved slowly in the darkness, with Rebecca wedged between them. The way back seemed to take three times as long with Rebecca gasping in pain between them.

When they reached the incline Ashby looked at Nic. There was no easy way to lift her without touching her back and Rebecca was barely standing as it was, she would never be able to walk up that.

"Nic you're the tallest, you'll have to put me over your shoulder," Rebecca said looking up the slick hill.

"Are you sure?" he asked.

"No, but we're out of options."

"I'll go first and pull you as we go," Ashby offered.

Nic nodded then gently lifted Rebecca up over his shoulder. Ashby started up the incline and reached back for his best friend. "We can do this," he said encouragingly.

"Don't feel bad Nic, I get to stare at your butt," Rebecca said, weakly.

Ashby sniffled and smiled. Rebecca's humor got them moving. Carefully, as they could not afford to fall and drop their injured Alpha Mother, both he and Nic made their way to the top.

In the distance, twilight made the exit glow with the soft white light of the moon. Once they were on firm footing Nic eased Rebecca down to stand on her own two feet.

"I need a weapon," Rebecca whispered her eyes filling with fear when a hyena's cackle filled the air.

Ashby watched shocked as Nic reached behind him and pulled a gun from his waistband. Wordlessly he handed it to their Alpha Mother.

She looked down at the gun in her hand and nodded slowly. "They all have to die." She met their eyes. "They said they were coming for the children," she said her voice sounding stronger.

Ashby straightened. "We're with you no matter what," he promised.

Rebecca nodded, then looked out toward the woods and the sounds of the fighting. An inhuman roar reverberated through the trees. She gave a soft smile. "That's Aleks."

"Come on Alpha Mother, the Arkadion is waiting for you," Ashby said taking her free hand.

Nic took a defensive position in front of them, despite being unarmed.

Another roar had Rebecca chuckling, then gasping in pain. "He's always so loud."

"TMI," Nic said in a deadpan voice.

Ashby stopped when Rebecca did, she clutched at her blanket and tried desperately not to laugh. "Owww it hurts." She grinned up at them. "Nic, you're awesome."

He winked at her. "Come on."

Ashby felt as though Rebecca's pain filled laughter had somehow began to thaw the icy fear that had surrounded his heart in her absence. As long as they had Rebecca, he knew they'd be okay.

"Aleks, you're being loud again," a soft voice said from behind him. Aleks spun around. Rebecca was walking slowly, supported on either side by Ashby and Nicholas. A rough wool blanket was wrapped around her naked body, and rivulets of dried blood covered her arms and legs. He ran to her and dropped to his knees in front of her. He wrapped his arms around her carefully and buried his face in her chest. He couldn't hold back his tears.

"The bastards had her chained in one of the mine shafts in a pool of ammonia to mask her scent. I bet he wasn't counting on Nic and I being able to sense her," Ashby said, staying close to Rebecca.

"I'm okay. I'm okay," Rebecca kept repeating.

"Aleks, step back, son, let me look at her," Dr. Claybourne said. Aleks shook his head unable to move.

"Aleks, if she's hurt, I need to make it so she's not in any pain. You don't want your mate in any pain, do you?" the doctor asked in a very calm voice.

Aleks shook his head and leaned back.

"Are you hurt?" he asked Rebecca gently then stood. He pulled the blanket back carefully. The wool fibers stuck to her back, and she cried out when it was removed. Dr. Claybourne immediately covered her front with a sheet. Aleks stood shaking with the need to destroy.

"Who are you working with?" Bran demanded, punching the hyena in the face again. The hyena just laughed.

"Take me to Arkadia, put me in jail and I will tell you all I know. The clients, the routes, everything," he said, spitting blood on the ground.

Grinding his canines, together Aleks looked at Bran and then Liam. He knew that they wanted to taste this man's blood, shake his body apart and watch his life slip away as much as he did.

He looked back over to Bran, and the wolf Alpha gave a terse nod. It would be worth the sacrifice to get information. Aleks turned back and was shocked to see Rebecca standing before the prisoner holding the sheet around her. Out of the folds of the sheet, she brought her right arm up pointing a gun to his head.

"Poor, little human. I have already made a deal with the Arkadion," the hyena said and cackled.

"Poor, little hyena. I'm the Alpha Mother and I haven't agreed to shit. It will be a cold day in hell before I let you anywhere close to where my children will be. You will never, ever get them, or any of Arkadia's children" she said flatly and then pulled the trigger.

At such close proximity the back of the hyena's head exploded outward and his body fell. Rebecca continued to shoot his body until all of the bullets were gone. The sound of the gun's clicking filled the night air as the gunshots echoed off of the trees. Everyone stared at the tiny woman in the middle of the circle. Rebecca looked up and saw that two hyenas were being held, one by a wolf and one by a lion.

"Kill them," she said softly.

"Yes, Alpha Mother," the men replied in unison and ripped the heads off the hyenas they had been holding.

Rebecca looked up and Aleks flinched at her cold gaze.

"Aleks, I want to go home now," she said softly. Swallowing hard, he stepped forward, lifted her up careful of her injured back, and carried her to the SUV. It was time to go home.

CHAPTER EIGHTEEN

"ALEKS, I CAN WALK," REBECCA said for what felt like the one hundredth time as Aleks carried her into the diner. It had been over a month since Aleks brought her home after her kidnapping. She kept catching him look at her as if she would suddenly meltdown. The odd part was she was convinced that her violent side was a turn on for him. Weird.

He sat her down at the counter. Everyone began speaking in subdued voices. Word of what happened with the hyenas had made it around town, and now everyone was walking on eggshells around her. The only ones who treated her normally were Ma, Kate, Ashby, and Nicholas. Rebecca sighed. She had had enough.

"Are you okay, baby?" Aleks asked when he heard her sigh.

"I'm fine! You hear that, everyone, I am fine! Hunky dory, peachy, totally and utterly fine!" she said loudly to everyone in the diner. "I got kidnapped, stripped naked and whipped, which believe me, hurt like a son of a bitch. But I am healing. So please stop acting weird around me. I can't take it anymore!" she yelled.

"Oh sweetie, we're not worried about your physical injuries, we're worried about your mental state. You killed that man execution style. We just want to make sure you're okay," Liam said, coming up behind her and giving her a gentle hug.

"Is that all? All this time y'all have been acting as if I were about to go all postal on your asses because of that?" Rebecca started laughing.

Kate smiled. "I told y'all she was fine. I would have done the same thing and it wouldn't have bothered me one bit. But I wouldn't have shot him. I would have ripped him apart with my canines starting with his groin," Kate said. Bran and the rest of the men winced. Unlike Rebecca slow recovery, Kate's wolf had her up and around much quicker than her human friend.

"I also told you to act normal, but you didn't listen to me," Ma said, handing Rebecca a cup of coffee.

"We expect it out of you and Kate, Ma, but Rebecca is so..." Connor started but then caught the eye of all three women.

"I'm so what, Connor?" Rebecca challenged.

"Itty-bitty," he replied flatly. There was silence.

Rebecca, then Kate started laughing. The atmosphere in the diner changed and brightened.

"I may be itty-bitty, but no one, and I do mean no one, threatens my children or this town. If they do, they die," Rebecca said simply, blowing on her coffee. The men just stared.

"He threatened our children?" Aleks asked, growling and grabbing Rebecca to put her in his lap, which seemed to be a growing habit with him. He wasn't happy unless he had her in his arms at all times.

"Watch my coffee," she said, growling when he jostled her mug.

"There's that tiny growl I love," Ashby said, walking into the diner with Nicholas. "Have they started acting normal yet?" Ashby asked, walking up to kiss her on the cheek.

"Yup, evidently they thought I was unbalanced," Rebecca said, holding her coffee to her chest. She turned to Aleks. "Yes, they said that even if I escaped they were going to figure out a way into town and wait until I was pregnant and then cut me open and take our son," she said, giving a sniffle. "I wish I could shoot him all over again!" Rebecca exclaimed. Aleks just nodded.

"Speaking of which, where on earth did you get that gun?" Liam asked.

"Nic gave it to me," she said, taking another sip of coffee. All eyes swung to Nic, who shrugged.

"I got it from Roman, Gabriel's acting second-in-command. I told him I needed something so that I could help in the fight. I like a nine millimeter."

"I'm sorry I couldn't let him live to get information. I just couldn't chance him escaping," Rebecca said to the group quietly.

"Don't worry, Rebecca. Gabriel said they are still working on the hyena that we captured trying to get away at the mine. He's slowly getting more information," Rian said with an evil grin.

"I know a lot of people are rethinking their views on smaller shifters thanks to you, Ashby.

Your size worked to our advantage, and you never stopped trying to save Rebecca. That took a lot of courage," Ma said, smiling at Ashby.

"I would do it again too, except maybe the being naked in the snow. I swear I froze my..." He looked around and cleared his throat. "I was cold," he said, blushing. Everyone laughed.

"Okay, now that everyone is acting normal, there's something I need to do," Kate said, standing. She looked down at Bran, who nodded and smiled. Kate walked over to Rebecca and took her coffee, placing it on the counter before taking her hands.

"Rebecca, I don't remember much from that night at the club, but I do distinctly remember you jumping in front of the hyena who was about to stab me in the heart. You put yourself in harm's way to keep me safe. You have also shown that you can think and plan, even when getting tortured, and that you are willing to do whatever it takes to keep our children and our town safe. I'd like to offer you my allegiance." She knelt down and tilted her head in a submissive manner. Ma gasped. By showing submission, Rebecca knew that Kate, and through her Bran, was giving her the pack.

Rebecca's eyes filled with tears. She slid off of Aleks's lap and placed both hands on Kate's shoulders.

"You are the sister I never had. I swear to always take care of you and the ones you hold dear," she said before placing her lips on Kate's neck. Both women sighed happily.

"Dude, that was hot!" Emmett exclaimed. Pa reached out and cuffed him upside the head.

Rebecca and Kate looked at each other and

laughed. Rebecca went to help Kate stand until both women realized that it wasn't going to work and they started laughing again. Rolling his eyes, Aleks offered Kate a hand up.

"I'm so happy. Everyone is safe and acting normal! Whoo hoo," Rebecca said, dancing around the diner. "Come on, Aleks, it's time for my doctor's appointment," she said, heading to the door.

"But you've already had your stitches out," he said as she jumped up and down trying to ring the diner's bell. She paused and looked at him.

"It's not for stitches. I get the results back from my pregnancy test today," she said matter-of-factly, tilting her head.

Aleks blinked once, then twice before his eyes rolled up in his head. Liam jumped out of the way as Aleks went down and hit the floor. Her eyes went wide before she threw both hands in the air and started dancing around as if she were boxing.

"Yes! Yes! Yes! And round one goes to Rebecca. It's a KO, ladies and gentleman." She danced around until Liam, laughing, picked her up and swung her around like a doll.

Rebecca laughed. She knew being human she'd have to do whatever she could to keep her bear guessing, it was the only way to keep the upperhand. Looking down at her unconscious mate she knew that she was off to a great start.

EPILOGUE

"WE LOST THE GIRL." THE hyena whined cowering in fear. The gentleman spun from where he was looking out the window and frowned.

"That makes me sad. Had you not gotten greedy and demanded the entire town, the Arkadion would have probably given you his blood," he said in a perfectly cultured voice. The hyena started to shake.

"If you lose control of your bladder on my antique Turkish rug, I really will kill you. As it is, I'll need to air it out to get rid of your stench from groveling on it." He paused, tapping his chin. "Now there's an idea. Payne," he called out.

The dark figure stepped from the shadows.

"Make a note that for future meetings with the hyenas that they stand on plastic. It will keep both of us from ruining the carpet. I had to replace the last one when I tickled his spine," he said grimacing.

The figure nodded.

"Please don't kill me," the hyena begged.

"I almost forgot you were there, old boy. Yes, the girl. We will try for her again later. I have a new target for you." He smiled brightly down at the shaking hyena.

"There are twin infant boys in Arkadia. Their blood is most rare, almost completely gone from this world. I want them. Bring them to me." He nodded to Payne and the man stepped forward.

He reached down and dragged the hyena out the room who began screeching in fear. The gentleman smiled, turned his back on his guest, and resumed looking out the window. He smiled as he watched a hawk swoop down and carry off a squealing rabbit.

"The oldest law in the world, survival of the fittest, predator eats prey," he said to himself.

He went back to his desk and looked down at the files stacked to one side. He fanned them out looking at each name before smiling. "Poor, poor bastards. They have no idea that they're no longer the predator, they're now prey." Chuckling he went back to his window.

Thank you for reading!

I hoped you enjoyed FATE KNOWS BEST! For a full listing of all my books please check out my Official Website www.alaneaalder.com

I love to hear from readers so please feel free to follow me on Facebook , Twitter, Goodreads, AmazonCentral or Pinterest.

Hug me please!!

SEND ALANEA A HUG!

LEAVE A REVIEW

If you liked this book please let others know. Most people will trust a friend's opinion more than any ad. Also make sure to leave a review. I love to read what y'all have to say and find out what your favorite parts were. I always read your reviews.

IMPORTANT!!

As you know Facebook strictly controls what shows up on your newsfeed. To ensure that you are receiving all my latest news and teasers you can to sign up for my newsletters so you will receive regular updates concerning release information, promotions, random giveaways and future Live events.

THE ALANEA CHRONICLES

Volume I, Issue I

March 2014

I typically send only 1-2 updates per month and won't flood your inbox, promise! ;)

Other Books by Alanea Alder

KINDRED OF ARKADIA SERIES

This series is about a shifter only town coming together as pack, pride, and sloth to defend the ones they love. Each book tells the story of a new couple or triad coming together and the hardships they face not only in their own Fated mating, but also in keeping their town safe against an unknown threat that looms just out of sight.

Book 1- Fate Knows Best
Book 2- Fated to Be Family
Book 3- Fated For Forever
Book 4- Fated Forgiveness
Book 5- Fated Healing
Book 6- Fated Surrender
Book 7- Gifts of Fate
Book 8- Fated Redemption

BEWITCHED AND BEWILDERED SERIES
She's been Bewitched and he's Bewildered...

When the topic of grandchildren comes up during a weekly sewing circle, the matriarchs of the founding families seek out the witch Elder to scry to see if their sons' have mates. They are shocked to discover that many of their sons' mates are out in the world and many are human!

Fearing that their future daughters-in-law will end up dead before being claimed and providing them with grandchildren to spoil, they convince their own mates that something must be done. After gathering all of the warriors together in a fake award ceremony, the witch Elder casts a spell to pull the warrior's mates to them, whether they want it or not.

Each book will revolve around a unit warrior member finding his destined mate, and the challenges and dangers they face in trying to uncover the reason why ferals are working together for the first time in their history to kill off members of the paranormal community.

THE VANGUARD

We Hold the Line.

Book 1- Inception

Printed in Poland
by Amazon Fulfillment
Poland Sp. z o.o., Wrocław